Acknowledgments

A very special thank you to **Cindy Goldrick** for her comments and suggestions on the final manuscript. I truly appreciate the time you took to read and re-read all those words.

Thanks to Margherita and Jack for keeping me technologically updated.

Thanks to Shirley, Barb, Adela, Kirsten, Ron, Rick, John, Peter and all the staff at SPINNAKERS on the harborfront in Toronto.

And thanks to Lady D for the swimming and the lessons.

Author's Note

DIVE MASTER, set along the Gold Coast of Florida and the Keys, is a stunning read. For anyone who has gone or wanted to go to South Florida they will quickly recognize and appreciate the intriguing murder mystery that develops there.

The next book, L.A.—set in Hollywood and the surrounding area will also include Monika Queller as the main protagonist. For late breaking information visit the web site:

www.pathcom.com/~munsey

I hope you enjoy all the Monika Queller™ mystery books as much as I enjoy writing them.

Terence

In the mirror reflecting tall,
I wonder if it's me at all…

For Apollo

Prologue

Through the darkness of the clear night sky, the full moon brightly shone upon the ocean waters. Its light reflected upon the water like a million dancing fireflies. Surprisingly the incoming tide was very rough even this far out from shore, with its powerful menacing swells. The moonlight unevenly covered this motion.

The night was cool for this time of year, though much warmer than the freezing temperatures that drew the many snowbirds from the North to winter on these southern Florida shores. From a distance, out into the warm waters of the Gulf Stream, the glow and activity on land could easily be seen, but the sound of the waves cresting and the wind blowing drowned out all other sound.

Upon these waters about a mile or so offshore floated a large unkempt ship. It was a trawler of some sort that, in the darkness of the night, silhouetted by the light of the large full moon cascading over the water, sailed with a majesty and pride that it no longer knew in the daylight hours. Quietly it travelled parallel to the coastline on a heading that was taking it farther south, towards the Keys.

"Hey. Stop," came a cry from within the ship.

Suddenly the wheel of a watertight door on the starboard deck-side turned. Three men —one Caucasian, young, in his late twenties, with slender build and blond hair; the other two of Latin origin, older, in their fifties and stocky, dirty looking 'salts' —appeared through the open door. They were engaged in a struggle. The two Latin looking men were forcing the Caucasian man through the door, out of the ship and onto the deck.

"Shut up," one of the Latin men spoke as he held onto the Caucasian man's left arm. He held a half-smoked cigar within his clenched teeth. "You're gonna ruin my cigar." He laughed.

"What's going on?" The Caucasian begged to know an answer as to why he was being brought out on deck so late, though deep inside he was afraid to hear what he sensed to be the reason.

The question was left unanswered as the two

men who were overpowering the younger man made their way the fifteen or so paces from the doorway to the ship's rusty seaward railing. One of the men roughly turned the young Caucasian around and pushed him back onto the railing.

"You're going for a swim," the man with the cigar continued, responding to his question.

"This far out? I can't."

The two men grinned. That was the point. Without further comment, the men lifted and pushed the younger man higher onto the railing. There was a tremendous struggle. The younger man kicked and screamed in an effort to avoid what he clearly knew would be his fate if he was thrown overboard this far from shore in these rough waters. He fought hard with strength far beyond his normal ability. Hope rose up in him as he managed to hold himself against them and prevent being tossed over. He seemed to be winning the battle. Then, one of the men, growing tired of the effort and the game, pulled a large metal object out of his back pocket. With one quick and powerful blow, he brought the metal object down hard onto the left side of the younger man's head. The young man flinched in pain and then went limp. Blood oozed from the side of his head.

"Come on. We've wasted enough time on this already," the man with the cigar, out of breath, grated out to his comrade. "Let's finish this."

The two men lifted the unconscious man higher

and then pushed him over the railing. They watched as he fell. By the time he hit the water, the ship had travelled twenty or thirty feet forward. Through the glitter of the moonlight, amidst the choppy ocean, the man's body splashed into the deep water and disappeared from sight. The men chuckled and turned away. Their job was done. Now they could report and go back to their normal duties.

The shock of hitting the cold water roused the young man from his unconsciousness. He immediately opened his eyes and discovered that he was submerged in the ocean. Becoming acutely aware of all his senses, he felt the rush of adrenaline through his body. He felt a throbbing on the side of his head and the sting of the salt water against an open wound. He was being twisted and turned in the water by the current of the ocean and the power of the ship passing. He realized that he must try to swim away quickly or risk being sucked into the ship's strong propellers. The ship's hull was about ten feet away from him, and the stern was rapidly approaching. He could hear and feel the loud noise of the propellers twisting in the water not far from him. Then he began to experience the strength of their pull.

With great effort, he began to swim. He needed to get out of the pull of the propellers and get to air. He pulled with his arms as he kicked his legs. It was a hard effort, his clothes and shoes weigh-

ing him down. He mustered all his strength in the
effort to escape the pull of the ship.

Stroke after stroke, kick after kick, gradually he
moved through the water. He was making
progress. Soon he pulled himself up from beneath
the water. He yelled out as he surfaced and drew
in a deep breath of life saving air. Quickly he submerged himself again and pulled off his shoes and
socks, resurfacing seconds later. The stern of the
ship was almost upon him. He turned away and
started to swim harder, away from the vessel. He
did not look back, but kept pulling himself
through the water. Now that his shoes and socks
were gone, he was making better speed.

By the time the stern of the ship was upon him,
he was far enough away to be out of danger. The
ship passed by, leaving him unharmed. Realizing
that he was safe from the pull of the ship, he
stopped swimming and turned to watch the vessel
as it sailed away southward. On the back of the
stern painted in large black lettering was the
name: C O N D O R A and under it in smaller letters: KEY WEST.

A sudden jab of pain ripped through his head.
Now that the danger from the ship was gone and
his adrenaline was diminishing, he could feel his
wound. He brought a hand out of the water to
probe the depth of the gash. Flinching in pain, he
brought his hand back and saw that it was stained
red. He was losing a lot of blood. He had to stop

it, but there was nothing he could do here in the ocean. He wondered if there might be any sharks lurking below the water—if they might be near enough to get the sent of him, if… he wiped the thought from his mind. There was nothing he could do about it so there was no point worrying.

He turned in the water and caught a glimpse of the glitter emanating from the shore. There were many lights. The beauty of their sparkle and variety of color upon the water struck him. It was fortunate he had not been thrown overboard in a more desolate and wilder stretch of the coastline.

His thoughts returned to sharks, and for a brief moment, alligators, but he believed that he was too far out in the ocean to be threatened by those reptiles. He cringed at the thought of them. He was probably safe in this more populated area of coastal water.

The shore was about a mile away. He was not sure if he could manage the distance or if the loss of blood would allow him to arrive safely at the beach, but he had no alternative. Determinedly he began to swim for the lights on the shoreline.

After half an hour the effort of the swim was becoming tremendous. The water was rough, and the swell of the waves about four feet. Swimming down the swells was easy, but managing his way back up the next one while going in a straight route to shore was harder. He was becoming weaker with every stroke he took. The pain from his head was growing and the wound was still raw.

As he swam, he began to drift in and out of lucid thought. He did not remember who he was or where he was from, or even why he had been on that ship. This struck him as odd. He re-focused on the effort of the swim. He could not stop: if he did, he would drown. He was tiring, and still far from shore. The desperation of his situation struck him. But he could not stop…

- - - - - - - - - - - - - - -

"Cap'em. It's taken care of," the Latin man with the cigar announced as he and his comrade made their way into the wheelhouse of the CONDORA.

The wheelhouse was, compared to the rest of the ship, the cleanest and most well kept area. It was a large space that had a commanding view of the ship and the ocean. On either side of the room there was a wide watertight door with large glass portholes. The front of the room consisted of large square plate glass windows that were placed at an angle and rose from the three-foot steel wall of the wheelhouse to its ceiling. The windows ran along the entire front and provided the most inspiring unobstructed view.

In the center of the room was a large ship's wheel. It was crafted of a dark wood and had highly polished brass fittings. It was mounted on a strong looking brass tower. There were instruments clustered around and above the wheel.

Beyond it was a counter that skirted the main windows. Scattered across the counter were charts and other papers.

Behind the counter and wheel were two large captain's chairs, reminiscent of swivel chairs from an old time barber's shop. Directly behind the chairs, about five feet away, was a sparsely decorated steel wall displaying a picture of the CONDORA taken in better days and a brass plaque with something that was written in what appeared to be Spanish.

There were three uniformed men in the wheelhouse. They were wearing the clothes of the United States Coast Guard. They were each clean cut and appeared in top physical condition. One, in his thirties, with dark hair and skin, was holding onto the ship's wheel, checking the ship's compass that was placed immediately in front of him. He was focussed upon his duty watching out over the dark ocean outside, as he steered the vessel. Another, in his late thirties and balding, was bent over the counter to the left of the wheel examining the charts. The other, in his forties, with a full head of light shortly cut, was sitting in the Captain's chair overseeing them, with a stern expression

'That's good, gentlemen. You may return to your duties below," he said matter-of-factly.

"Yes, Cap'em." The men turned, opened the door and exited, pleased that they had done their job well.

"Mr. Whelen," the Captain directed his words to the black man at the wheel.

"Yes Sir," Whelen formally and quickly responded.

"Keep her steady."

"Yes Sir, Captain." Whelen kept focussed.

"Mr. Faling."

"Sir." Faling turned and looked up from his charts toward the captain.

"You have the con." The Captain rose from his chair as he spoke. He went over to the door on the other side of the wheelhouse and opened it.

"Sir." Faling crossed over and, before the captain had left the room, got up in his chair.

The captain closed the door and walked the few steps along a narrow steel gangplank to another door. He opened it and entered. It was a small room. Inside a single seaman was sitting in front of the ship's communication center. He had headphones on. Upon seeing the Captain he removed the headphones.

"Sir." The seaman, in his late teens and obviously a fresh recruit, readied to stand and salute.

"As you were," the Captain ordered.

"Yes, Sir." The seaman relaxed.

"I want you to send a message to the base."

"Yes Sir." The seaman turned and prepared to send a coded message.

"Cargo off at Ft. Lauderdale. ETA 0900." The

Captain paused.

"Sir?" the seaman questioned, thinking the message was not finished.

"That's all son. Get that off and sign it CONDORA. Inform me of any reply." The Captain turned and left.

"Yes Sir."

The Captain walked down the steel gangplank heading for his quarters. He needed a break. He didn't like this sort of business, but he was under strict orders, orders that he had followed before and was now too deeply involved with to extricate himself. He needed a drink.

- - - - - - - - - - - - - - -

Knock. Knock. Knock. Three rapid knocks sounded upon the door.

"Come," was shouted from inside.

The office door opened and a young Coast Guard lieutenant entered.

"Sir. We've just gotten a message from CONDORA."

This was the office of Major Britin, commander of this small Special Ops base in Key West. It was a spartan room with one large metal table, a couple of filing cabinets and a US flag standing in the left corner. There was a large curtainless window behind the Major.

"Don't just stand there Corporal. Let me have it," the Major commanded.

The Corporal hurried over to Britin and handed

him the note. He stood back and waited as the Major opened the message.

"That'll be all." The Major did not look up, but read the note.

"Sir." The Corporal saluted, turned and, as he left, closed the door.

"So it goes again. Poor bastard." Britin mumbled to himself as he finished the message. He threw the paper on his desk and reached for his phone. He dialed a number and waited while the phone rang. Britin's assistant in the outer office answered.

"Lieutenant."

"Yes Sir."

"Send Alpha Team up to Ft. Lauderdale. It's a routine clean up."

"Yes Sir. Right away." The lieutenant hung up.

Major Britin dialed another number. After several rings a man answered.

"Hello?"

Britin instantly recognized the voice. "Sir. The CONDORA reports its mission is completed." He paused and listened.

"Where?" was all that was asked.

"Off Ft. Lauderdale," Britin answered.

"Then we'd better send a clean up team to make sure the loose ends, if there are any, are tidied up."

"Yes Sir. I've already seen to it."

"Good work Major." The man hung up the phone.

Britin hung up the receiver and went back to his other duties.

- - - - - - - - - - - - - - - - -

He couldn't stop, but he was very tired and weak. As he swam it was getting harder to remain afloat. He swallowed some water and began to choke. He was no longer able fight the current of the incoming tide. He was a quarter of a mile off shore. The CONDORA was out of sight. He was beginning to give up his fight and accept his fate. He no longer felt the pain from his wound, nor the coldness of the water. He was being pushed and pulled by the current and the waves. Periodically, as he rode up a wave swell, he caught a glimpse of the sparkling shore lights—they reminded him of Christmas lights. He was saddened as he realized that he would not see Christmas again. This thought spurred him on to one final spurt of energy, but it was not enough. He did not have the strength. The loss of blood had greatly diminished him. He began to drift in his consciousness. He kept swimming. He kept swallowing more and more water with each breath he drew amidst the chop of the water. He tried to strengthen his resolve, but it was just too much for him to accomplish. If he had not been hurt, he might have had a chance. He did not want to die. He was too young. There was so much more he had hoped and planned to do. He began to repeat to himself that he must not stop. He must not stop. He must not…

On this third repetition he slowed his stroke. His arms and legs lost their power. His muscles became limp and uncontrollable. Against his will, his body stopped swimming. It was too much for him. He was physically and emotionally spent. He could go no further even though he wanted to. His weary body had reached its breaking point. It was only a matter of a few moments and it would all be over.

He reconciled himself to his destiny. He began to sink below the surface. He did not try to take another breath. It did not matter to him whether he survived two or three minutes more or less. He had tried his best and could go no further. There was no hope left to him.

A sudden wave of despair and acceptance overpowered him. He took in a breath, but it was filled with water and not air. He breathed in and out in a fish-like action. He could find no air to sustain himself. He gagged. He gave in to the ocean and finally, he succumbed.

Chapter 1

"Good morning," Monika called out to another patron of the Riverside Resort as she closed her door and started down the curved flight of stairs from her second story efficiency.

"Good morning." The other patron continued on to his room on the same floor.

The Riverside Resort was a quaint place situated right next to the Intracoastal Waterway at Pompano Beach. It was a beautiful small resort with a capacity for about forty quests. It was larger than a bed and breakfast, but smaller than a regular hotel. Monika had stumbled upon this little piece of paradise thanks to a friend who always vacationed here.

The resort walls were painted a clean white and the site was fashioned in the adobe architectural style, which was accented by its flat roof. The whole structure was built in a U shape that formed an inner courtyard facing the Intracoastal Waterway. The courtyard contained a beautiful green lawn, hibiscus trees in an array of flowering colors—red, yellow, orange —their aroma permeating the warm tropical air, a small grove of banana trees on the southern most edge of the property, several palms trees of differing shapes, sizes and varieties and a heated kidney-shaped swimming pool—though there was no need to heat a pool at this time of year. The pool sparkled in the bright morning sun.

There were only two stories to the Riverside, which added to its picturesqueness. A large verandah ran along both floors. Its balustrade was made of wrought iron and in a Spanish motif. Each room had its own little kitchenette and looked out over the courtyard onto the Waterway, where there was constant activity. Boats of all shapes and designs were constantly sailing up and down. One could make a vacation of just sitting on the dock of the resort and watching the boats. It was an incredible sight to view the millions of dollars that went by non-stop. Though there was a lot of activity on the Waterway, it was amazingly peaceful here in the courtyard and at the resort. There was so much to distract the senses and soothe. It truly was a paradise.

Monika took all this in as she began to descend the stairs to the courtyard and exit the resort en route to the beach, which was a short walk away, about a quarter of a mile east of the resort. Monika was only staying there the night and wanted to have a pleasant uninterrupted day at the beach before she continued her trip south through the Keys. She had arrived the night before in Miami airport. It had been a very late flight by Florida standards, but she had still been on California time and did not feel tired—for her it was three hours earlier. She had rented a compact car and then made the drive up to the Riverside and Pompano Beach.

Pompano Beach was a quiet community about ten or so minutes north of Ft. Lauderdale. It was right on the beach and the Intracoastal Waterway and provided a peaceful vacation spot. It had all the amenities. Though a sedate town, if she wanted more action all she had to do was drive the short distance to Ft. Lauderdale to be immersed in its non-stop partying. But that was not what she wanted on this trip.

Upon her arrival at the Riverside the manager, a friendly French Canadian woman, had waited up for her and helped her settle in. The Riverside was more like a beautiful home —friendly, safe and loving— than a hotel, and the manager reminded Monika of an old caring aunt.

This morning Monika awoke refreshed and quickly dressed for the beach. A white flowing top loosely buttoned at her tiny waist, just covered her bikini. She had on dainty tan Italian sandals and a pair of small oval shaped designer mirror-blue sunglasses that complimented her flowing blond hair and angular face. She carried a large beach bag made out of tan raffia in her right hand, which contained everything she would need at the beach.

Arriving at the bottom of the stairs, she paused a moment to admire the sight and take in the sweet smells; then she continued through the courtyard over the sprinkler wet grass to the exit and the secondary roadway that would lead her to the beach. It was 10:00 AM and there was no one else around.

Monika made her way out through the resort and onto the side street that the Riverside fronted. There was not much activity, probably because this was a Sunday morning and people were recovering from a busy Saturday night. She looked down the street ahead of her and could see in the distance the path that led to the ocean. She started walking along the side of the road. It was going to be a typical Florida day. The sky was azure blue with a few fluffy clouds and the sun was bright and warm—much warmer than her home in Santa Barbara at this time of year.

The street was made of tar and pebbles, not the

cement and curbs of regular roads. It reminded
her of the roads of a small rural town. Along both
sides toward the beach path, were little private
cottages that were obviously kept as summer or
weekend places. Each cottage was clean and had
the most abundant gardens. Even the more
neglected cottage was well kept and had a garden
that was lush. Monika noted the array of flowers,
green plants, and colors. Everything looked so
fresh. Unlike California, there was a lot of water
here that was used to keep the vegetation fresh.

As she walked, she also noted the change of
scent from cottage garden to cottage garden. All
of this beauty relaxed her, and within two or three
minutes she had arrived at a path, which was a
narrow, sandy, well-trodden public access to the
beach. It was about three feet wide and ran
between two cottages that faced the ocean. On
either side of the path was a white-washed six-
foot stucco wall overgrown with a green plant that
resembled ivy. Monika stopped. About thirty feet
away was the beach and the ocean. She suddenly
became aware of the soothing sounds of the
waves hitting the beach and the light warm breeze
caressing the sandy shore. She sighed.

"Now this is more like it," she said out loud to
herself and smiled. Nothing else in time existed
for her now. Her life in Santa Barbara was gone.
She willingly let it go and dived into a world of
sensory existence: a place where she didn't have

to think; a place where only her comfort and passions mattered. She felt a tingle go through her and her skin raised with goose-bumps. She intended to be selfish and pamper herself. She was going to make this the best vacation she had ever had.

Leaving the roadway she started upon the path. It was difficult to walk in the sand. Monika stopped and removed her sandals. The feel of the warm sand beneath her feet was sensual. She smiled and walked on.

At the end of the path lay the beach and the ocean. The beach was a very light tan color with fine grain sand. Monika walked straight from the public access toward the gently rolling ocean. The water was, like the vegetation, colorful and evocative. The fresh sea air was invigorating.

Along the shore where the tide rose and fell, the sand was a darker tan from the salty wetness of the surf. The water ranged from a green-tan, turquoise, light sky blue, at the shore radiating fifty yards out, to an ever-intensifying color of blue and turquoise, 'til finally a deep dark blue marked the horizon.

There were a few people scattered on the sand. The beach was about seventy-five feet deep. At the top it was skirted by private cottages and low story condominiums painted in whites, pinks and yellows. They were not at odds with the scenery and ran the length of the beach.

To the north, about a mile away, an automated metal tower lighthouse jutted out into the ocean.

To the south about a half a mile away was the Pompano Beach Pier. The pier was built of heavy wood that had weathered to a dark brown. At the end of the pier about a hundred yards out into the ocean, there was a small covered structure. Monika thought that she might investigate it later in the day, but now she would soak up some sun.

Satisfied, Monika walked further along the beach and chose a spot about twenty feet from the water to set up her blanket and relax. She threw her sandals down along with her beach bag and pulled out a large white beach blanket. The blanket was the size of a double bed sheet, she preferred to have a large beach blanket to lie on.

Carefully she spread the blanket out over the sand. The light breeze from the ocean blew up a corner so Monika decided to weigh each corner of the blanket down with a small pile of sand. She then placed her bag on the blanket and removed her top, revealing her slim figure which was barely covered by a tiny and feminine floral patterned bikini. She was truly a pretty picture on the beach, but she drew no attention, as there was hardly anyone there to notice. Monika appreciated this. She did not want to be bothered, ogled, or hit upon, though she felt like being pretty today.

She pulled out her sun tan oil and began to rub it over her skin, starting with her legs and then moving to her arms. The oil was warm and silky and made her feel soft. She sat down on the blanket and rubbed it onto her stomach and the exposed skin around her bikini top. She tried to get some on her back, but could not reach it. Finally she lightly patted some on her face around her sunglasses. Finishing, she put the lid back on the oil and placed it back in her bag. Other than her sunglasses and a diamond engagement ring on her left forefinger, she wore no other jewelry. There was nothing to worry about losing. She lay back on the blanket, closed her eyes and relaxed.

As she lay there, she felt the warmth of the sun intensify on her. The warm breeze of the ocean and the gentle rhythmic sound of the surf cresting and falling upon the sandy beach caressed her ears. Waves of pleasure began to pulsate throughout her. It was an orgasmic experience. She had clearly needed this escape, needed to relax.

Her mind began to drift. She began to imagine herself with a strange man on the beach. She was lying on the beach and he, a muscular blond-haired man in his early thirties was coming out from the surf. He had on a small black European bathing suit that clung tightly to him. His taut stomach and chest dripped with water; his powerful legs carried him through the shallow surf. He brushed his hair out of his face and wiped away the water. He was fixated on her. His green eyes probed her depths. Monika relaxed more and felt herself soften in anticipation of him joining her.

As he strode up the beach, she propped herself up on both her elbows behind her back and watched him. He was still dripping as he came up to her and fell down onto the blanket beside her. She coyly complained, but really liked it. She was excited by his presence. She felt her heart skip a beat and then increase its rhythm. They were talking and joking, but she couldn't make out the actual words. They were just having fun. She felt his hand upon her left thigh as he caressed and moved up her. She fell back onto her blanket as she opened up to him and he was leaning over top of her. His hard body pressed against her. She felt the soft warm sand beneath her, and the warm sun on top of her. He kissed her. Waves of passion crested and fell within her. She felt the insistent heat of his hardness pushing against her. She responded by kissing him harder twisting her body more closely to his. She pulled backward and reached for his swimming suit and pulled it down to feel him suddenly exposed against her. She felt his hand move to spread an opening in her bikini bottoms and she guided his excited manhood into her. She opened herself to him to allow his total entry between her…

Monika was suddenly jarred from her daydream by a shower of sand.

"Hey?!" She opened her eyes and looked around to see who had disturbed her from her fantasy.

"Sorry." A little girl and her brother were hurrying past her, and apologized for kicking sand upon her.

"Kids," Monika thought to herself. "Whatever happened to respect for others."

Monika sat up. She realized that she must have dozed off for a while. The beach was becoming more crowded. She drew in a deep breath and sighed. "What a dream," she announced to herself. "Where did that come from?"

Monika was engaged to James, and happy. She wondered why she would have such an erotic daydream. It didn't disturb her, but she found it curious that she would have such an explicit fantasy. She chuckled and shook it off. It was probably a result of all the sensory input that she had experienced since her arrival in Florida.

Feeling a little warm, she got up from her blanket, brushed off the sand that had been kicked on her by the passing-by kids and crossed over to the water.

Slowly she entered the surf. The water was warmer than she expected. Though the ocean was fairly calm there was a slight undulation and the small surf created by the waves splashed against her legs. Her feet sank into the sand as the surf rolled in and out. She remained a moment and surveyed the surf up the beach. A rippling white line of surf continued as far as she could see towards the lighthouse. The roll of the ocean was powerful and constant; the sound of the crashing water upon the beach prominent.

There were a few other people in the water up and down the beach. There were tiny children with pails and plastic miniature shovels playing in the sand along the surf, and other using floatation devices playing in the shallow water along the shore. There were a few adults farther out into the water away from the busyness of the shoreline, and then a few families just standing with their feet in the water enjoying their vacations.

Monika moved further into the water, step by step. With each step the water rose higher up her legs. Though it was not too cold, it was still a shock to her and she went slowly until she was brave enough, and in deep enough water, to finally dive in and submerge herself. She had not removed her sunglasses and was careful not to lose them in the water.

The ocean water was soft and very salty. When she resurfaced she carefully wiped the hair out of her glasses and face and continued breast stoking through the water. The smell of the salt water was clean and fresh. After a couple of minutes Monika was about thirty yards from shore and in deeper water. She was not able to touch bottom, but could see the sandy ocean floor through the crystal clear water. There was no plant life or rocks, just sand. She thought she saw a small fish quickly swim away, having been disturbed by her presence.

Monika was enjoying herself. It had been a good choice to come ahead of James for a few days on her own: a mini vacation before she met up with him in Key West. James' parents had a place there and she was going with him to meet them for the first time. James was flying in directly to Key West later in the week. She would meet him at the airport and together they would spend a week with his parents. Monika would have these few days before, to travel and explore Florida from Pompano on down through the Keys. She had always wanted to make this journey on her own and was excitedly anticipating it.

Monika paddled in the water and admired the view of the shoreline from the pier to the lighthouse. She decided to remain here a few moments longer and then make her way back to the beach. Everything was so peaceful and beautiful. She was not aware that this serenity was about to be broken. She was not yet aware of her vulnerability out here far from the safety of the beach. She was not aware of what was slowly approaching from behind in the deeper open waters.

As she tread water something was approaching her. It was slowly and stealthily making its way. There was no escape. With each roll of the waves it came closer. It was large and hovered just below the surface. Monika was facing the shore and had not yet seen it. Within moments it would be upon her.

Chapter 2

"Are we on schedule?" asked an elderly man seated in a small conference room in the old and now abandoned naval base in Key West. He was in his early nineties, well dressed in an expensive dark gray suit, white shirt and conservative tie. Though old and frail, he still had a nerdy look about him. He was sitting at the head of the conference table. This was William Fence, one of the richest men in the world. He had made his fortune years ago in the burgeoning computer software industry. His company, Microtech, had always dominated the industry and, despite attempts by the government to curb his power in what they called a monopoly, it and he had survived and prospered.

Originally Microtech had focused upon the user end of computer software, but as the company grew it began to expand into other major areas of research and development. Now Microtech was much more than a software company. It had holdings and subsidiaries throughout the world in almost every industry, including the medical research industry.

"Yes Sir. We're still on schedule and ready for Friday. Everything will be in place." A uniformed man, Colonel Charles Brookland, a veteran of the army spoke confidently. He was in his forties, clean cut, mid brown thinning hair, glasses, and a little on the fat side for a career military man.

"And what about the…" Fence looked down to some papers in a folder in front of him checking a particular report to make sure he used the correct terminology, "…Dive Master, Major Britin?" Fence turned his attention to the Major who was sitting to the right at the table. "Will there be any problems?"

The Major's tone was confident, "None at all Sir. We have the clone in place and he is completely under our control. He'll be arriving at Jefferson Thursday. Everything has worked perfectly. It all depends on the President not changing his itinerary at the Fort."

"Mr. Hemings?" Fence immediately turned to his right and directed his question to Cedric Hemings.

Hemings, a man in his forties, was good looking and dark haired with rugged features and a mustache. He wore a slim fitting simple black suit, starched white shirt and a narrow dark nondescript tie. He smiled before he spoke, indicating he understood what Major Britin was trying to do. Both he and Britin disliked and mistrusted each other. There was a healthy competition between them to out-do or embarrass the other whenever possible, which found its origin more in the history and jealousy between their respective professional organizations than in their personal prejudices. Britin was an army man and Hemings a Secret Service agent attached to the White House. In particular, Hemings was assigned to help plan the security arrangements for some of the President's special domestic appearances. Like the one that was about to be made at Fort Jefferson.

"No. The President is looking forward to his underwater swim. He used to scuba dive a lot before he got into politics. He never gets a chance these days. That's the part of this trip he's looking forward to, not the ceremony to put a plaque on a historic site," he chuckled. "As long as this Dive Master doesn't screw-up, the switch can be easily made. If the clone is as good as you say, then no one will suspect a thing." Hemings baited Britin.

It was the secret joint partnership between the military and Microtech that had originally begun the research into cloning and replacement technology, known as CART. The military was researching cloning in the hope of using the technology to raise a generation of disposable soldiers. Microtech had stumbled upon a method of synchronous human-machine interactivity that would allow direct brain machine contact and control—the perfect hands-free operating system.

Through this technological development, Microtech had inadvertently discovered a method to upload and download not only machine data to human, but also human data to machine memory. In essence a person's complete memory, with all his or her knowledge and experiences, could be downloaded and saved. The military hadn't realized the possible ramifications of this new development. It was Microtech that made the initial link. Now it would be possible to not only physically clone another human being, but to duplicate the actual inner thinking person to within 99.9% as well. Only .01%, the 'soul', of the actual person was beyond their reach to download. It was a mystery yet to be solved but it was of no immediate importance to them. For all intents and purposes it would be possible to live forever. Though a clone may have its own soul, all the other aspects that would make it a real person's duplicate could be uploaded from storage as many times as desired. From the military's point of view, they would be able to manipulate not only the genetics in cloning a soldier, but also adjust and control the personality. It was a major break-through.

The military and Microtech worked together to test and develop this technology and pushed it beyond its initial scope. It did not take long for Microtech and a select group within the military partnership to realize the other potentials of this technology. Not only could you in essence live forever, but you could also control all the important political and business leaders in the world by CART cloning. All that was needed was a genetic sample to rapidly clone the person, and enough time to download the complete memory. With the improvements and discoveries that CART made, physical cloning could be accomplished in weeks from a tiny sample, and memory cloning in about half an hour.

Another man, wearing a short-sleeved blue shirt with a white plastic pocket protector, tie, and glasses, Dr. Vernon Pearl, (a man from the deep south who had a slow southern drawl to his speech) was sitting at the table. He picked up his cue to speak. This was his area of expertise, being the chief scientist at Microtech assigned to the cloning project.

"All we'll need is about half an hour. We can make the initial switch underwater. The plan is to take the President, download his memory at Fort Jefferson and upload it into the primary clone. As far as the world will know, the primary clone in the water will have an accident and lose consciousness. Because help is at least seventy-five miles away at the Key West Naval Hospital, and if Hemings and Britin have done their job, we will be able to use the makeshift infirmary at the Fort. I will be able make the transfer as long as I have enough time."

"Don't worry about me. I'll have the President's helicopter." Major Britin took offense at the doctor's innuendo.

"And there won't be any other air support on Fort Jefferson. The rest of the President's security will travel by boat along with the media. This occasion isn't seen as an international trip and fewer precautions have been taken. It will take half an hour to scramble from Boca Chica Naval Air Station and land there. By then you should have everything under control. Within forty-five minutes of the event the President will be back on his helicopter and flying off the island." Hemings had meticulously planned every aspect of the itinerary of the switch and was confident of its outcome. He was part of the White House planning staff and would not be on the island. Someone else not involved with the plot would be in charge of the field group. It was safer that way.

Once the President dove under the water at the fort, their plan would be put into motion. It would be hard to see into the murky water of the fort's moat. This would hide the switching of the clone for the President. There was an old submerged drain, which led from the moat to the infirmary on the lower level of the fort. The President would be taken there. For the plot to work, it relied upon the precision work and timing of the entire team.

"It will be tight," Dr. Pearl commented.

"But can you do it?" Fence demanded reassurance.

"Yes. But I need at least half an hour. Twenty minutes at the very least." Dr. Pearl was adamant.

There was a silent pause as each of them at the table regarded each other, wondering who would stick their neck out and guarantee, in front of William Fence, the successful outcome of the mission.

"You'll have your half hour Doctor," Hemings spoke and through eye contact gave each of the others at the table his affirmation. "And we'll…," he acknowledged their stares, "have our President."

Chapter 3

Monika turned to face out into the open water. Something inside her suddenly made her feel uneasy. As she paddled she scanned the water in her vicinity. She saw nothing unusual. She decided to turn and swim back to shore having been, in her mind, in the water long enough.

She began to swim toward the beach with a little more speed than her more casual swim out. Instead of doing the breaststroke, she now used the crawl. She pulled at the water and kicked her feet, her head submerged and twisting every other stroke for breath, her hand stretched out and pulling at the water in front of her. The salty water made her more buoyant than the regular chlorinated public swimming pool she was used to and she was making good speed. For some reason she was afraid. She thought it strange to have this sudden emotion. Her mind heightened her senses.

Suddenly Monika bumped into something in the water. She immediately stopped dead in the water. Adrenaline began to surge throughout her. She pulled her head up, screamed and nervously muttered a few incoherent words of fear. She began to tread water and move backward from whatever she had hit. Her senses focused upon the spot in the water where she had collided with the object. Seeing nothing, she waited a moment, twisting her head in all directions scanning the water. She felt exposed and vulnerable, unable to touch bottom.

Then something in front of her about five feet away bobbed up and remained floating at the surface. Monika recoiled. She was not sure what it was, but instinctively understood that it was not a shark or other dangerous fish. It had a strange familiarity to it. She considered it to be some sort of large ocean jellyfish that had somehow drifted out from the deeper water to the shallower water at shore. But after several moments of observation she realized it wasn't.

Feeling a little braver she ventured toward the floating object. It seemed to be some sort of creature. Because it was moving, Monika was beginning to accept that it presented no danger to her.

As she examined its half-submerged shape, she began to make a guess at its possible identification. She wondered what it was or wasn't. It was clearly some sort of creature, but it was too limp and motionless to be alive.

Cautiously, and barely in command of her fear and flight reaction, she swam closer. As she came to within three feet of the creature, a large wave rolled through and twisted the creature up and over to reveal the partially bloated face and head of a blond-haired man. Monika screamed uncontrollably and became hysterical as she again recoiled.

"HELP! Somebody help!" she screamed out and began to swim away from the body to shore. She was only twenty yards from the beach.

The loud screaming could easily be heard on the beach. The wind from the ocean helping to carry her voice farther. Several people were now standing up and looking out to where all the commotion was coming from. Once they identified the source, they started shouting out to the lifeguard, but he had already seen the disturbance and, after having confirmed the problem through his binoculars, jumped down from his tower, a hundred or so feet farther south along the Pompano beach, and was running to rescue the troubled female swimmer. As he ran he was making note of the water surrounding the female for the possible cause of her obvious hysteria. He saw the large floating object, which by now was a fair distance away from her.

"Everyone out of the water," he yelled and waved his hands to those in the vicinity as he entered the surf. Making large leaps he soon was into the deeper water away from the shore and swimming out to Monika. Within seconds their combined efforts brought them together.

"What's wrong? Are you hurt?" the lifeguard shouted to her as he approached.

"A body! There!" Monika was hysterical, but relieved that the lifeguard was there to protect her. She continued to swim until she managed to touch bottom. Touching terra firma, along with the guard's presence, began to quiet her panic, but she still desperately wanted to get out of the water and back to the safety of the beach.

The lifeguard looked over to the object that was now closer to him. It was definitely a body and he could tell from his experience and the level of decomposition caused by the salt water, that the body had been in the water for several hours. It would not be a pleasant sight. He did not like the idea of dealing with a dead body in the water.

"Okay. Okay. Don't worry. It's okay," he spoke slowly and calmly. "Are you okay?"

"Yes. I'm...I'm...okay. Just a little scared," Monika blurted. She was out of breath from the swim and the shock. "It was awful."

"I know. But you're okay now. Let me help."

The lifeguard, now touching bottom, crossed to help Monika to the beach.

Monika felt his firm grip on her, and noted his strong muscular body, as he helped guide her the remaining few feet from the surf to the beach. She felt weak-kneed from the ordeal.

As they both came out of the water, the guard had to support Monika's weight. He lifted her up and carried her out of the surf onto the beach. A small crowd had gathered and surrounded them. He gently laid her on the sand.

"What's your name?" the guard asked.

"Monika." She was still in shock, but very relieved to be out of the ocean.

"I'm Skip. Hi. That was quite a scare, but you're okay now. Just relax. I'll take care of you."

Monika paid attention. Skip was in his twenties, sun tanned weathered skin, warm blue eyes and sun bleached long hair. He had a pair of sunglasses secured around his neck with a multicolored neon string. There was neon pink sun block on his nose. She did not respond, but continued to observe.

"Everybody back. Give her some room." Skip looked up and spoke to the crowd that was huddled around.

"Okay everybody. The show's over. Let's clear away." Another lifeguard, female and bossy, Skip's partner, now arrived as back-up at the scene. She was making her way through the crowd to Skip to check on the situation. As she came through the crowd she called out to Skip. "What've we got?"

Skip stood up and spoke in a quieter tone, "A floater in the water. You'd better call it in."

"Oh," his partner grunted out disapprovingly. Even she didn't like floaters. "Okay. Need any help here?" she said, quickly changing the subject.

"No. Go ahead. I'll help her over to headquarters in a minute. She's okay. Just scared. Needs to catch her breath."

"You bet," she nervously chuckled, turned and made her way through the remaining people that were standing by and watching.

Skip knelt back down to Monika and asked, "Let's get you to headquarters. It's just down the beach. We can get you a coffee. There's going to be some paperwork I need to fill out."

"Sure. Just give me a hand." Monika was recovered, but reflective. She wondered who the man in the water was and how he had come to be there. It was terribly sad. She felt sympathy for him. A chill ran up her as she recalled seeing his face. Beyond the water damage, she could tell that he had been a young and handsome man. She shook herself, realizing that it would be a long time before she forgot that face.

"Here. Take my hand," Skip offered.

As Monika stood up he put his arm around her

to comfort her. Ignoring the remaining onlookers, they both began to slowly walk down the beach.

"My things." Monika remembered her blanket and bag on the beach. She stopped and reconnoitered the beach. "There. They're over there." She pointed out a spot about fifty feet down the beach in the direction they were going. The ocean tide had pushed her farther than she had imagined.

"No problem. We'll get them on the way," Skip noted and then changed the subject. "So, Monika do you live in Pompano or are you just visiting?"

"I'm from Santa Barbara. Here on vacation," she started. "I'm meeting my fiancé in Key West at the end of the week," she added this just to be on the safe side. She didn't want Skip to get the impression she was available.

"Oh…and what do you do in Santa Barbara?" He didn't show any reaction to her obvious notification. He wasn't interested in her. He was just making conversation and trying to distract her thoughts.

"I teach."

"Teach? You look too young to be a teacher." Skip smiled. Monika returned his smile and accepted his compliment.

- - - - - - - - - - - - - - -

About half an hour later in front of the lifeguard headquarters, Monika was standing with a large blanket wrapped around her, sipping coffee. Though it was warm out, she felt chilled. There was a bustling of activity in the area. The police and coroner had arrived and the body was out of the water and resting in a lifeguard dory waiting to be removed.

"Ms. Queller?"

"Yes."

"I'm Detective Casteño of the Pompano police. You found the body?" A short suave-looking man of Cuban-American descent, came over to her.

"Yes," Monika said matter-of-factly.

"Do you mind if I ask you some questions." He was being very polite.

"No."

"I know this must have been awful for you. Skip has already told me some of the details, but there are just a few more routine questions."

"Okay." The reality of the morning's events had sobered Monika out of her vacation and thrown her into a more reflective mood.

"I understand you're a teacher?"

"Yeah. High school."

"Oh," he smiled and nodded. He was standing next to her.

As they spoke they both watched a group of men lifting the large black plastic body bag out of the dory and place it on a stretcher to be carried off the beach and into the coroner's station wagon.

"You're here on vacation?"

"Yes." She was tired of all the questions that

had been asked of her since finding the body.

"Married?"

"What?"

"Are you married?"

"No. Engaged." She didn't understand why the detective was asking. Her defenses went up.

"Oh. Congratulations."

She didn't respond.

"Are you here alone?"

"Yes. I'm meeting my fiancé in Key West at the end of the week."

"Skip says you were swimming and bumped into the…" He did not say the word, but pointed, indicating the body on the stretcher that was now being carried by the men up the beach. "Could you tell me everything?"

Monika frowned and let out a sigh. "I was on the beach sun tanning and decided to go into the water to cool off. So I went in and swam out from shore. I was swimming around and then there it was." She grimaced at the thought.

"1625 Garden Lane, in Santa Barbara. Your current address?" Casteño pushed forward in his investigation without reacting to her discomfort.

"Yes."

"What are your plans here?"

"I'm going to go to Key Largo tomorrow to see the underwater park. I was going to spend a day in Miami sightseeing, and then make my way down through the Keys and take in the sights.

Then meet James at the airport in Key West."

"James is your fiancé?"

"Yes."

"Your first time in Florida?"

"No. I came once before to Ft. Lauderdale during spring break, but that was years ago." Monika decided to be more cooperative. The detective had a job to do. It wasn't personal.

"Sounds like you're going to have a busy week. I'm sorry this had to happen."

"Me too."

"Well. I think that's it. Sorry to make you repeat everything. I don't think we will need to ask anything more, but if we need to, we'll contact you in California."

As the detective finished, the men carrying the body came up the beach and passed within six feet of them, heading for their car which was parked in the lot beside the lifeguard station. Monika and the detective fell silent until they had passed. The bag was zippered closed but they could see the jiggling of the body as the men walked. The sight intensified the already horrific event.

"Will you be able to find out who it was?" Monika asked.

"I hope so. But it will take a few weeks. He didn't have any identification, and his fingers are badly decomposed. Fingerprinting won't be possible."

"How do you think it happened?"

"I'm not sure, but he had a terrible gash on the side of his head. Maybe he fell off a ship."

"Fell off a ship?"

"Sometimes we get illegals in these waters."

"Illegals?"

"Yeah. People trying to get into the States without papers. The people they deal with aren't very scrupulous." He saw her disgust. "But maybe it was just an accident of some sort. Who knows? It will take a while to sort out."

"Oh."

"Please don't worry. We'll solve it. You're in no danger. Tell you what. If I find out anything today, I'll call you at your hotel. Okay?"

Monika smiled. "Thanks. I'd appreciate that."

"Well." The detective had all he wanted and prepared to leave. "I've got to ask the coroner a few questions. Thanks for all your help."

"I didn't really help much."

"Can I get anyone to take you anywhere?"

"No. Thanks. I'll just walk back to the hotel. I think I'll spend some time at the pool."

The detective grinned. He understood her meaning. "Well bye then. I hope the rest of your vacation is great. And congratulations on your engagement."

"Thank you."

"Call him," he added this personal touch, meaning that she should call her fiancé. They shook each other's hand and he left.

During all this time, unbeknownst to Monika, a man, sitting in a dark blue late model car, had been watching her. He had also snapped several pictures using a digital camera with a high-powered telephoto lens. He plugged a cord from the camera into a small laptop and within seconds the photos he had taken popped up on the screen. The laptop was connected to a terminal centrally located in the lower dashboard. He typed in several commands, highlighted one of the pictures that was best suited for his purpose, and then pressed the enter key and waited.

Several seconds went by and the terminal connected using the car's communications capabilities via satellite link to an outside database. It was all very high tech. Several more seconds passed and the screen went blank and then a file with Monika's photograph popped up. It was her driver's license information out of California. All the information was accurate. She had been identified.

The man saved the page and then took out his sat-phone, a mobile phone that used a telecommunication satellite to make calls, instead of the regular cellular ground technology. He pressed in a number and waited.

- - - - - - - - - - - - - - - -

The phone in the abandoned naval base conference room rang just as Hemings finished his sentence. Everyone became silent as Major Britin took out his sat-phone.

"Yes." Britin was business-like and short. He listened as his man in Pompano spoke.

"Report."

Again he listened.

"What's her name?"

There was a brief answer.

"Can you uplink that to me here?"

Britin nodded at the reply.

"Good work Corporal. Keep her in sight and report anything unusual." Britin took the phone away from his ear and terminated the call by flipping the phone closed. He put the small black phone back into his jacket pocket.

"It seems, Colonel, that we have a glitch in our plan. It appears that a young woman, a Monika Queller, found our Dive Master on Pompano Beach. The local authorities have the body, it was just pulled out of the water."

"Colonel?" Fence sounded annoyed.

"It doesn't matter. He has no prints and no dental history. There's no way that he can be identified or traced."

"I thought you said he would never wash up on shore," Fence's tone was accusing.

"It's unusual, but it won't affect the plan. The body isn't traceable. We made sure of that." The Colonel didn't appear to be at all nervous at this turn of events. He would have preferred that the body had been lost at sea, like the others that they had disposed of along the coast, but it really would not make any difference.

"You'd better be right," Fence threatened.

"There's no problem. These situations have all been prepared for." The Colonel took the threat to heart. "Major," he ordered Britin to explain.

"We will keep the girl under surveillance. If anything is suspicious, she'll be silenced. There's already a team in place."

"Good." Fence was placated. "Let's not have any more glitches. We've worked too hard for this opportunity to waste it on some oversight. Is everything else ready?"

Britin began first. "Yes Sir. My men know only that they are assigned to add back-up to the Secret Service on the island. We will arrive Wednesday with them by boat to do all the preliminaries. They will be in place and are on need-to-know."

"I've taken Command personally of the forces in the Keys. No one will do a thing without my clearance. This will give us more time if we should need it. And the base here is still off limits to all personnel," the Colonel added.

"My team will coordinate with Britin's. As far as they're concerned, it's just a standard mission. They don't suspect a thing," Hemings continued.

"There's no problem at my end. Just get me that half hour." The doctor was last to speak.

"Good. Then gentlemen, the next time I see you

all, we should be in control of the nation, and no one but us will know anything has changed. To our success." Fence stood up on these last three words.

"Success," the others replied in unison.

- - - - - - - - - - - - - - -

Monika returned to the hotel and went to her room to get her cell phone. She sat down on the bed and dialed James' number. The phone in California rang. It was just after eight in the morning there.

"Hello?" A groggy sounding James answered.

"Hi sweetie. Do you miss me?"

"Monika. I was just dreaming about you," James teased. He was happy to hear from her and know that she had arrived safely. He had intended to call her later, but felt comforted that she had not waited, and called him first.

There was silence on Monika's end. James' mood changed.

"What's wrong?" He sensed that something was wrong.

The sound of James' voice broke down the barrier of strength she'd been hiding behind. She became emotional and a little teary. It was the release that she had needed and one that only James could have given her.

"I found a body in the water." Her voice broke as her emotions overtook her.

"Are you okay?" James was worried. Monika

smiled and felt comforted as the sound of James' familiar voice rolled over her, but she needed a moment to compose herself. She could not respond immediately.

"Monika? Are you okay?" James understood her emotions, and probed in a very gentle tone.

"Yeah. I'm okay. Don't worry." She composed herself. "It was just a bit of a shock."

"What happened?"

"I went for a swim and bumped into a dead man in the ocean. I've been talking to the police and lifeguards all morning."

"Oh. I'm sorry you went through all that. It isn't a nice way to start a vacation." James understood what it was like to stumble across a body. It was never a welcome experience even in his line of work with the CIA.

"No... It wasn't." Monika became a little girl again. She was teary and needed James to comfort her.

"I can come earlier if you want. I could be there tomorrow?" James offered.

"No. That's okay. I mean. I'd like to see you, but I'm okay. I just miss you."

"Are you sure?"

"Yep. Really." Monika forced her voice to remain strong. "I'm okay. I just needed to hear your voice."

"Why don't you stay by the pool and relax today. I'll call you later to see how you're doing.

Okay?"

"Okay." Monika felt weepy again, but hid it from James by keeping her answer short.

"I love you." James recognized the vulnerable tone in her voice. He had an incredible urge to put his arms around her and protect her.

"Love you too," Monika returned.

"Bye."

"Bye." She ended the call and sat on the bed trying to compose herself. It had been an awful start to her vacation.

- - - - - - - - - - - - - - -

"Mr. President. There's the Fort Jefferson date on Friday, noon."

In the Oval Office of the White House, the President was going over his upcoming schedule for the week with his secretary. He always did this on Sunday morning before he and his family went to worship. He was a young man to be President, in his late forties, good looking with dark hair. He was debonair. He had been a newly graduated lawyer, a Stanford graduate, when he had run for and won his first political office. From Grand Rapids, Michigan, he had married his college sweetheart and now had three teenage children, two girls and a boy. He was happily married and was the poster-boy for good American family values.

His political career had rocketed forward and within twenty years he now found himself in his first term in the highest office in the land. Not only was he a personally popular first term President, but he was also a respected veteran.

"Oh yeah. The Florida Keys. It should be nice this time of year. That's the one I'm looking forward to." He had a warm friendliness to his voice.

"Yes Sir. There's some diving on this one." His secretary, a cheery rotund black woman in her thirties, smiled. She knew that his casual answer was a rouse. He had been looking forward to this appearance for weeks, like a young schoolboy, anxious to go on holiday and have fun.

The President smiled. "You know me too well, Connetta." He knew that she had seen through his attempt to minimize his interest in this trip.

"Yes Sir." Connetta stood in front of the desk where the President was seated.

"Anything else that day?"

"Yes. You have the American Song Awards dinner that night."

"Damn. It would have been nice to spend the night in the Keys. The First Lady would have liked that."

Connetta smiled and nodded her acknowledgment to his rhetorical statement. She wished they could stay also. She liked the President and First Lady.

- - - - - - - - - - - - - - - -

All that day the Corporal sat in his car in the heat watching Monika's hotel. He had seen her go into the main courtyard entrance. He knew this particular hotel well and knew that the only other exit she could take would be via water taxi on the Intracoastal Waterway. He had requested back up to watch from the Waterway. All he could do now was to follow his orders and wait until she appeared again. He was hot and uncomfortable. He could not leave the car running all day to use the air conditioning, so he had rolled down the windows and suffered the heat.

Monika was lying on a reclining patio chair on the hotel's deck along the Intracoastal Waterway. She was relaxed again. Speaking with James had helped her put the incident of the morning behind her. She watched the boats go up and down the Waterway. There were all manner of boats passing. The manager had chatted with her earlier and told her that there was always a parade on the Waterway at Christmas. All the boats were decorated with Christmas lights and sailed along the Waterway. It was an incredible sight that, if she ever returned, she should try and see. Other than the manager, Monika was not approached by any of the other guests who were, like herself, relaxing and taking in the sun. The Riverside was beautifully located. She would enjoy the rest of the day relaxing and start off early in the morning for Key Largo Coral Reef Reserve. Hopefully she could restart her vacation there.

All along the Waterway were private houses

with their own boat moorings. It was not unusual
to see people working on their boats or just sitting
in the sun. This area around the Riverside had
some of the nicest Waterway homes. Directly
opposite was a white two-story adobe house with
an in-ground pool. Adjacent to it there was a pink
ranch style bungalow. It also had a large swimming pool. Monika thought it interesting that in
an area within half a mile of the most beautiful
beach in the world, there were so many swimming pools, though after her recent experience
she began to appreciate it.

Several large cabin cruisers and a couple of
forty-foot sailboats were moored in and away
from the main Waterway, in what was obviously a
'water' driveway for each house and their respective boats, or ships. These were not the normal
'boats' that regular people owned.

About one hundred yards across on the other
side of the Waterway, a small powerboat was
moored alongside one of the larger cruisers.
Though tiny, it was not out of place. On board a
man, a young sergeant attached to Britin's unit,
casually dressed in shorts and an athletic shirt,
sunglasses and a ball cap, was sitting in the driver's seat with his feet propped up. He was sipping from a can of beer. This was the Corporal's
back up. Like the Corporal, he had a sat-phone
and a pair of binoculars, which he periodically
used to observe Monika lying on the hotel deck,

and to check-in with the Corporal on the other side of the Riverside. He enjoyed this aspect of his military career—spying on a beautiful, scantily clad woman.

His orders were the same as the Corporal's. He did not know or care to find out the reason for the surveillance. He was just following orders. That was his job and why he joined up. He was trained and used to doing whatever he was told without question. What did he care if the brass wanted him to sit all day on a boat drinking beer and watching a woman. It was fine by him. There were worse things he could be assigned to.

Monika stretched and got out of her chair. The sergeant on the small boat observed her actions more closely. She picked up her towel and other belongings and proceeded to leave the courtyard and go up the stairs to her room.

The sergeant followed her every move with his powerful binoculars. He watched as she got to, unlocked and opened her room door, entered and closed it behind her. He moved his binoculars across to her window. There was a set of light sheer curtains. Monika came into view. She started to undress.

"Whoa! Come on darling." He watched as she began to remove her top. Just as she was about to reveal more, a huge hundred-foot cruiser passed in front and blocked the binoculars.

"Damn!" he exclaimed. "Hurry up. Hurry up."

He kept his eyes glued to the binoculars and made a waving motion with his right hand that no one could see.

By the time the cruiser had passed by, Monika was gone from sight.

"Damn," was all the sergeant said as he pulled the binoculars away in disappointment.

Chapter 4

The morning was clear, sunny and warm. There was not a cloud in the sky. Monika had gotten up, dressed and packed just after nine. She put her bag in the rental car outside and parked closer to the hotel office. She was wearing a light summer dress and had on a one piece Florida colored bathing suit underneath. Her sunglasses were propped up in her full flowing blond hair. She was ready to checkout and begin her adventure to Key Largo.

Her plan was to follow the old Federal Highway as far as she could and slowly make her way along the winds and curves. She thought she would get a better view of the area by not taking I-95 or the Turnpike all the way. By lunchtime she expected to arrive at Key Largo. Once there she would find a scuba diving place and arrange to spend the day out on the reef. She was excited. She had always enjoyed scuba diving and had done a lot of it in California both in the ocean and the lakes. Though California had some interesting dives, nothing could compare with the coral reef dive at Key Largo. The water would be crystal clear, warm and limpid blue. At this time of year the water temperature should be in the high seventies, so she would not need a wet suit. She was looking forward to the day and the dive.

"Good morning," Monika greeted Mrs. Lacure, the manager as she entered through the main door of the office from the parking lot.

The office was small, about twelve by twelve, and though air-conditioned it was very smoky. It was attached to the small apartment that was a part of her arrangement for managing the place.

"Oh. You are off already?" Mrs. Lacure's French Canadian accent was evident.

"Yes. I'm off to Key Largo." Monika put her handbag on the counter in front of her.

"Oh it is lovely there now. You will be going to the coral reef?" she asked as she remained seated behind the counter, taking a puff from a half-smoked cigarette.

"Yes. I plan to spend the afternoon and then I'll stay somewhere local for the night. I'm in no rush. I might even take a second day there."

Monika didn't mind people smoking, but the air in this tiny room was too stale and close even for her liking. She wanted to hurry up the checkout procedure and get on her way.

"Where will you rent your diving gear?"

"I'll find something when I get there."

"I know someone there who is the best. I will give you his pamphlet." Mrs. Lacure got up and came around the counter to a stand beside Monika that displayed brochures and tourist information. She searched for and then picked two pamphlets from the display. "Here."

Monika took the pamphlets.

"His name is Jesse Ehrlich, but he goes by Jess. He is the best. You go to him and tell him Mrs. Lacure at the Riverside sent you. He will treat you good." Mrs. Lacure went back around behind the counter.

Monika took a quick glance at the pamphlet. JESS'S DIVE TOURS was printed on the front. In smaller print below it: specializing in reef dives. Full packages available. There was an address and a phone number and some color pictures of the coral reef. It looked beautiful.

"I know him for many years. He and my husband were friends. He was a Navy Seal."

Monika wasn't sure if Mrs. Lacure meant her husband or Jess. She assumed the latter. "That sounds good. I think I will."

"The other pamphlet is a nice little hotel, like

the Riverside, but not as nice." Mrs. Lacure smiled as she graciously recommended a competitor. "You will like it there."

"I'll check it out."

"And here is your bill." She handed Monika a slip of paper.

The total was exactly what Monika expected it to be. She pulled her wallet out of her bag, drew out her credit card and handed it to Mrs. Lacure.

"Thank you, Mrs. Lacure."

"You are welcome. I hope your stay there is uneventful." Though nothing was said, Mrs. Lacure knew all about the events of the previous day.

"Me too." Monika did not want to talk about it.

Mrs. Lacure took the card and ran it through the bank machine. In seconds the machine printed a sales slip. She took the print-out and gave it, with the card, to Monika. Monika signed it and gave it back. With cigarette in hand, Mrs. Lacure stapled a yellow copy of the slip to the bill and handed it back.

"And this is your copy."

"Thank you." Monika took the copy and folded it. She placed it in her wallet, returned the wallet to her bag and placed the bag over her left shoulder.

"Maybe we see you again soon."

"I hope so. Bye."

"Have a nice trip."

Monika turned and left the office. The fresh tropical scented air welcomed her.

Outside across the street the Corporal was watching. It had been a long uncomfortable night. He was happy there was finally some action. His partner, watching on the other side of the hotel from the Waterway, had kept him updated overnight but now that the girl was leaving, he alone would follow her. He hoped the girl would stop somewhere to eat so that he could also get a bite and a coffee. There was nothing in the immediate area so he had not been able to slip away earlier.

Monika got into her car, pulled down her sunglasses and started the vehicle. Checking her mirrors and familiarizing herself with the rental car she backed up and pulled out from the Riverside and drove down the street. As she passed by, the Corporal started his car and prepared to tail her.

Though she had a map from the rental car agency beside her, Monika knew where she was going. At the end of the street she turned right onto Ocean Boulevard. From studying the map the night before she had planned her route. The Corporal was not far behind. There was not much traffic. Monika had her windows rolled down and was enjoying the breeze and the magnificent summery sights.

To her left was the beach and then the ocean. There were palm trees and tropical vegetation lining the roadway all along the beachfront. The sun was glistening on a calm blue ocean. The surf gently cascading as far away as she could see. Though she had noticed before, the beauty of the Gold Coast was still incredible. She knew that she would come back here again often.

Ocean Boulevard continued to run along the beach. She left Pompano and came to Lauderdale-by-the-Sea. Soon she was leaving Lauderdale-by-the-Sea and entering the outskirts of Ft. Lauderdale. At this point, Ocean Boulevard changed names to Atlantic Boulevard. The name reminded Monika of Monopoly. She wondered if this was where the name in the game originated.

At Sunrise Boulevard, which ran due west through the center of Ft. Lauderdale about fifteen minutes away from her start in Pompano, Monika turned right and started to head away from the beach. She needed to cross the Intracoastal Waterway and get to Federal Highway, the old Highway 1. She also thought that she would stop for a coffee and donut before making her way along Federal. She liked the idea of being in Ft Lauderdale again. She recalled the area around Sunrise and Atlantic well. It brought back pleasant memories.

As she turned the car, she saw a small donut place just along Sunrise before the bridge to cross the Intracoastal. Quickly she signaled and pulled right into the lot and parked. She got out of the car and crossed the lot into the donut shop. Behind her the Corporal followed, and drove by her in the parking lot as she was getting out of her car. The Corporal parked a few spaces farther up and got out and followed her into the donut shop.

The donut shop was small and geared to take-out. It was so close to the ocean here that most of its customers preferred to sit outside and enjoy the view. It wasn't busy.

"Can I help you?" a pretty teenaged girl behind the counter asked. She was wearing a uniform and standing at a cash register.

"A coffee. Just cream…and a chocolate glazed donut, please." Monika placed her order.

"For here?" the girl routinely asked.

"To go," Monika responded.

Behind her in line was the Corporal. He was the only person behind her. He heard her place her order. She had a pleasant soft voice. He stared at her, admiring her good shape and looks. He wondered for a moment why he was assigned to follow such a pretty and innocent looking young woman.

"$1.75 please."

Monika handed over two one-dollar bills. The girl quickly made change and gave Monika a quarter back.

"Thank you." The girl immediately turned and prepared the order, placing both the donut and coffee, on which she had firmly put a plastic lid, into a small brown paper bag. She handed the package to Monika.

"Thank you," Monika replied as she took the bag. As she turned to leave she bumped into the Corporal.

"Oh… I'm sorry." She had a sparkle of life about her.

"No problem, ma'am." He felt exposed and awkward. He became tense. He had gotten too close to his prey. He tried to conceal his nervousness at being acknowledged by her.

Monika kept going. She thought it odd that a man about her same age would say ma'am to her, but paid no more attention to the incident. She hurried out the door and found a place to sit on a bench in front of the donut shop.

Without her realizing, the Corporal, now more cautious, kept his eye on her. He quickly placed and got his order and went out to his car. He sat and watched her from a distance.

Monika was enjoying her coffee. Opposite her across the road just before the bridge was a road that led to a park area. To her right, about two hundred yards away, was the beach and the ocean. Though the street was not busy with cars, there were lots of people dressed in beach attire carrying towels, bags, coolers and beach paraphernalia, walking along the sidewalk en route to the ocean. To her left was the massive Lift Bridge that spanned the Intracoastal Waterway.

Monika soon finished her coffee and donut. She soaked in the sun and warmth for few moments and then got up and crossed to her car. She noticed the Corporal several cars away, but only gave his being there a passing thought. He was probably just enjoying the day like she was.

She got in, started the car and pulled out of the parking lot onto Sunrise, heading west. She was going to travel on Federal, which was on the other side of the bridge, until she got to North Miami. From there she was going to get onto I-95 and find her way to the Turnpike near Miami International Airport. She did not want to take Federal and drive through downtown Miami. From I-95 and the Turnpike she would see what she wanted. She didn't feel safe on her own in Miami, nor did she want to go into a major city. She was on vacation and trying to get away from that hectic inner city life. At the end of the Turnpike, in Florida City, she would get back onto old Highway 1 and cross the first causeway into Key Largo and the beginning of the Florida Keys.

She drove over the bridge and found her way along Sunrise to Federal. Many pretty sights passed by as she drove. Monika continued to be astounded by the picturesqueness of South Florida. Within twenty minutes the scenery began to change. This was the only part of the drive so far she did not like. This was the beginning of

Miami. These outskirts were dingy and rough looking. She noted the fear within her. She would not like to be stranded here.

Eventually she found her way onto I-95 by-passing Miami and recognized the Miami Airport from her arrival a couple of days ago. I-95 was very busy. She stayed in the right lane and watched for directions to the turnpike.

After several miles she saw the sign and fol-lowed the exit ramp to the tollbooths of the turn-pike. She was on her way. It would not be much longer before she was far away from the madness of Miami and in the peaceful natural world of the Keys. She felt elated.

The Corporal had managed to keep a safe dis-tance from Monika without losing her. He also pulled off the freeway heading for the turnpike. He wondered where the girl was going. He had been told by the Lieutenant at his base in Key West that the President was arriving at Ft. Jefferson this week and that his assignment was part of the security blanket for his visit. He had wondered 'til now why he was following this girl. Why would a girl vacationing in Pompano Beach be a threat? But now that she was heading south into the Keys, a few days before the Presidential visit, he was becoming more suspicious.

- - - - - - - - - - - - - - -

The trip along the Turnpike had been short. Monika was now on Highway 1 and half way across the causeway over Barnes Sound. She would be in Key Largo within the hour. She had made good time and would be there by lunch. That would give her a chance to get something light to eat. After lunch she would go and find Mrs. Lacure's Jess.

Crossing the causeway brought Monika into a different world than the rest of South Florida. Suddenly the scenery was more primitive and natural. It was just as striking as Pompano and area, but in its own natural untouched way. The ocean was a palette of blues and greens. All along the shoreline palm trees abounded and there was a sense of peace. Monika was soothed by the atmosphere. Everything had a sense of the casual and there was a feeling of freedom that she could not explain but felt. The experience of driving so far from any shore on a road that was so isolated and placed so close to, and in the middle of, a vast body of water, was almost frightening. It made you think you might be in a boat and not a car, upon the ocean. The sun here was more powerful, reflected by the glistening surrounding ocean. The combination of water, sand and palm trees created a romantic paradise.

Monika noticed a sign posted along the causeway: Welcome to the Florida Keys. Welcome to Paradise. She smiled. Obviously she was not alone in her impression of this place.

Not long after the sign, the causeway ended and

Highway 1 touched the dry land of the first of the Florida Keys—Ocean Key. Key Largo was about twenty minutes along the highway between MM (mile marker) 110 and 87. Monika knew from her reading that every location in the Keys was measured by MM's the distance in miles from Key West to that marker.

In the Keys, Highway 1 was the major roadway. Compared to other major highways, it was really an elaborate two-lane paved pathway that was primitively constructed and barely allowed cars to tightly pass in either direction. It was the original and only thoroughfare through the Keys, made in a time before mass tourism and travel found its way to Florida.

The Keys were a series of small islands linked together by the highway to each other and ultimately the mainland. Some were so small that nothing could be built upon them, and others like Key Largo, Marathon and Key West contained small but thriving self-contained communities. The Keys seemed to be a haven for artists and those wanting a peace and undisturbed serenity that they could no longer find elsewhere in the continental United States. Monika was pleased to be here.

Arriving in Key Largo, Monika noticed a restaurant off the main highway. She turned onto the street noting it was called Seaside Avenue and immediately saw a small two-story Cape Cod style building. There was a large handpainted sign along its facade: Snapper's Ocean Front Raw Bar. She pulled into the parking lot of the restaurant deciding that it would be a good spot to stop and have lunch. It seemed a welcoming place with its white washed clapboard exterior and covered lower level verandah. It overlooked a breath taking view of the ocean. There were no more of the high rise buildings of the Golden Coast to be seen here, just small quaint buildings.

Behind her the Corporal followed. He had kept her in sight all the way from the turnpike in Miami. He pulled onto Seaside Avenue and parked a safe distance along the street. He watched as she got out of her car and went into the restaurant. Although he was hungry, he could not take the chance of being spotted again. He opened his car windows and turned off the engine. With the entrance of the restaurant in clear view, he made himself comfortable in his seat.

Chapter 5

A long narrow corridor lit only by one yellowing sixty watt bulb in the ceiling led to the brig below level at the abandoned Key West Naval base. It was an old solitary confinement jail that had not been used in many decades. It was built during a time when the treatment of prisoners was more draconian. Several rusty steel gray doors spaced about ten feet apart lined each side of the gloomy corridor. Each door was shut and there was a tiny six by eight-inch barred window at eye level centrally located on each door.

From the distance, the sound of heavy footsteps coming down the corridor was becoming audible. Gradually a man dressed in uniform could be seen walking out of the shadows, like a ghoul in a horror picture as he came more into the light. It was Major Britin. With him were two soldiers. They were coming closer and seemed to enjoy the dramatics of the scene.

Behind the door in the tiny cell that was positioned under the only working corridor light, a young tormented blonde haired man was lying on a dilapidated metal bed. The cell walls were constructed from old shale. It was damp and cramped. Other than the bed, there was a light in the ceiling that was protected by a steel cage—like the ones on naval vessels, and a makeshift toilet, which was comprised of a ten inch diameter black cast-iron pipe standing eighteen inches above the dirty cement floor. It was built into the corner opposite the bed for privacy. A choking rancid smell exuded from it. This was a disgusting place. The man did not react to the loud noise of the boot steps that suddenly disturbed his usually solitary and silent universe. He was exhausted and asleep.

The sound of the steps came to and stopped outside this solitary prisoner's cell. Still he did not react, but remained motionless on the hard bed. The click and clank of the door's lock mechanism being twisted and opened followed the rustling sound of keys. Then the screeching sound of the door's rusty hinges was heard as it was pulled open. The light from the corridor fell into the cell and helped to brighten it.

"Get up," Major Britin stood in the corridor and commanded. "The doctor needs you."

The prisoner, lying with his back to Britin, lay still, his arm covering his eyes.

"Come on. I haven't got all day. It will all be over soon." There was no reaction.

"Bring him," Britin nodded his head as he ordered the two soldiers. "He's coming whether he likes it or not. Drag him if you have to."

The two soldiers entered the cell and began to turn the prisoner over, pulling him from the bed. As he was turned his face came into view. It was Jess, Jesse Ehrlich.

Worn and obviously beaten, Jess did not assist the two soldiers. He was lifted from the bed and roughly grabbed by his arms. The two bulky soldiers, who looked like football players, began to drag him out of the cell. Jess's shoes made drag marks on the floor as he was manhandled.

"Bring him." Britin turned and started down the corridor back the way he had come. The two soldiers obeyed, dragging a semi-conscious Jess in tow. They all walked down the corridor and disappeared back into the dark shadows from which they had come.

Jess was brought from the jail to the lab on the main level of the base. The lab was a large brightly-lit clean room. You would never have expected that an area such as the jail could have existed in the same facility as the lab. There was all sorts of high tech computer and electrical equipment here. Three rows of florescent light fixtures ran the length of the thirty by twenty-foot space. There was a blackboard with all sorts of numbers and equations scribbled, like an eccentric research scientist's classroom, along one wall to the right, and cabinets with counter space along the two others. Directly in front, across from the door was a set of windows. The venetian blinds upon them were shut, giving a claustrophobic feel to the otherwise spacious room.

Jess was thrown into what appeared to be a dentist's chair and strapped in.

"I'll give him a stimulant." Dr. Pearl, who had been watching as the men entered the lab, stepped forward. Now that Jess was secured, he felt safe.

"Will he live?" Major Britin questioned.

"Yes. He's been through a lot, but he'll survive." Dr. Pearl had stuck a syringe into a vein in Jess's left arm, and was injecting the stimulant. "Wake up Mr. Ehrlich. Time to go to work. Wake up." He patted Jess's cheek with his left hand trying to rouse him. Jess moaned. The drug was having its effect.

"You two wait outside," Britin ordered the soldiers out.

"Yes Sir," they each replied and left. Only Britin and the doctor remained.

Jess moaned again and began to open his eyes.

"Good, Mr. Ehrlich. Welcome back," the doctor's tone was patronizing. "We have a few more things to do before we can let you go."

"Haven't you done enough, you bastard." Jess was becoming lucid.

"Now, now. Is that the way for the best Dive Master in Florida to speak. You won't get many new customers that way." Pearl grinned.

"What do you want now?" Jess, now fully awakened, changed the subject. "Why are you keeping me here?"

"Just a few tests, Mr. Ehrlich. That's all." Britin stepped forward.

"That's not what this is all about. You're not letting me out of here. Ever." Jess played a hunch.

The doctor had moved away and was searching through some equipment.

There was a pause while Britin considered. "You're right of course. You deserve the truth. You served your country well in the past. We owe you that at least."

"Owe me for what? Who are you working for?"

"Working for?" Britin relaxed and laughed. "This is far beyond your wildest dreams."

"Try me." Jess stared at Britin. "This facility hasn't been used by the military in years. It's been off limits. So you have to be working for someone pretty high up to get the clearances. Who else is involved?"

"You're in no position to demand anything." He

paused again. "This is about honor and duty. Something you should understand. This country has fallen to the mercy of political corruption and is being run by the limited self-interest of lobbyists. This is about regaining control. Reasserting the will of the American people."

"You sound nuts," Jess pushed.

"I would have expected better than that from you. But I see you don't get it. You've been too comfortable for too long."

"Then tell me."

"You see all this stuff here?" He turned and waved his arm to indicate the lab and all its equipment. "This is the future."

"So why do you need me?"

"Patience Mr. Ehrlich. I'll get to it. The doctor here has perfected a very unique technology."

"Improved the microwave oven?"

"Don't be stupid. This is much more than that."

The doctor having found what he was looking for came back over to Jess. He had several electrodes and a syringe. "This won't hurt a bit. Stay still."

Jess tried to struggle but he was too securely tied. The doctor pricked the needle into Jess's left temple.

"Ow! I thought you said it wouldn't hurt, you quack."

"Now Mr. Ehrlich it's just a little numbing. It will take hold soon. Don't be such a baby."

"What's going on? What are you going to do?"

"Just a little downloading. It won't hurt and will be over in minutes." The doctor tested Jess's temple for numbness and was satisfied that the local anesthetic had worked. He carefully inserted a series of fine acupuncture-like needles into Jess's temple and with them a microscopic computer chip just beneath the skin. "This little devise is the key to it all. It's really a remarkable piece of technology."

"What is it?"

"This will allow us to connect you up and download all your memory," Britin interjected. "It won't do any damage to you and it will give us everything you are and know."

"Why me?" Jess didn't understand his importance to these men. He was just a simple Dive Master running his own business in Key Largo. He was no longer involved in the military. He was just a private unimportant average citizen.

"You don't give yourself enough credit. You're about to become a very important man."

"Why?"

"On Friday you are going to help us abduct the President."

"The President? I won't do it."

"You're right. YOU won't do it, but you will." Britin laughed. Jess didn't. "You still don't get it, do you? On Friday you are going to guide the President on a dive at Ft. Jefferson in the moat.

We needed someone we knew. Someone close by. Someone we happened to have old DNA samples of. You were requested to report and being the best Dive Master in Florida, and an ex-seal, you had the proper clearance."

"DNA?"

"From that mission in the Gulf. You were wounded and treated, remember?"

"Yes, but…"

"We were starting research into developing a new breed of soldiers and we needed samples, samples that we could get without any questions being asked. We were experimenting and trying to perfect the technology."

"Technology for what?"

"Cloning," the doctor blurted.

"Cloning?" Jess was stupefied.

"Yes. We've managed to perfect the cloning process and add a few improvements to the process."

"You're going to clone me?"

"You weren't the only one. It just so happens that you are in the right place at the right time for the right opportunity. There are others, but they don't have your present qualifications. You're the top of the class."

"But I'm meant to be at Ft. Jefferson on Thursday?"

"No, no Mr. Ehrlich. You don't understand. You are slow. It makes me wonder if we've made the correct choice."

"I won't help you, and there isn't enough time."

"But you already have. This is just a very tiny part of the process. We cloned you a year ago."

"But that's not me. It's just my body. No one will be fooled."

"Wrong again. It doesn't look like Mr. Ehrlich is going to pass the test. Does it doctor." The doctor and Britin chuckled. "That's the improvement I was talking about. That has always been the greatest hurdle to overcome. The doctor here, along with others, has managed to leap over it."

"How?" Jess wanted to know more. If he was going to stop Britin, though he did not know how he was going to do it, he needed to know more details.

"Cloning has been available and perfected for quite some time now. We've managed to develop a technique that can attach a person directly to computer technology. No more need to physically type to enter or retrieve data. No need to verbally interact. Whatever you want, you can do by a direct link between brain and computer. It's an incredible leap. Imagine how it will improve society. All that is needed is a microscopic computer chip installed like the one in your forehead. Then by infrared waves a link is made. Like a wireless mouse on a computer. It's amazingly similar technology. The possibilities are endless. The upside to this advance is that now we can clone an exact duplicate of someone physically and also upload 99.9 percent of all their experiences, knowledge and memories. We can also make a few modifications in some instances, such as yours. The only thing we can't download is, for lack of a better term, your soul. But I'm sure we will eventually find a way, given enough time to explore this new frontier."

"You're mad." Jess was disgusted.

"Maybe, Mr. Ehrlich. Maybe. That's a moot point. But like it or not you are helping us, or rather your duplicate is."

"It will never work."

"You're right. We have had a few setbacks. We even had to get rid of a couple of your earlier prototypes, but we've worked out the bugs now. That's why we want one more download, as a back up, just to be on the safe side. In case something happens to you, the original." Britin gave a menacing glare.

"So what about the President?" Jess prodded. Britin seemed eager to tell all.

"That's the kicker. It so happens that we had a DNA sample from his military service and we've cloned him. Now all we need is to download his memory, and with some changes, we will be able to get this country back on line. It's very fortuitous. Everything has just fallen into place."

"You'll never get away with it. Someone will find out."

"You really don't understand this breakthrough, do you. We already have gotten away with it. All we need to do now is get hold of the President, download his memory, upload it into the clone and substitute the clone for him. All we need is a few minutes of the President's time in private. No one will suspect a thing. That's why we needed you. It's all worked out and in motion."

"And what if something goes wrong. Something short circuits in the clone?"

"We have spares. A quick secret exchange will take care of any problems, but we don't anticipate any. The duplication is practically perfect. Just like yours is."

Jess felt helpless. Britin and his co-conspirators, whoever they were, had obviously prepared well.

"So as you can see everything is going according to plan. On Thursday morning you, your clone, will arrive at Jefferson. When the President arrives you will do your duty and escort him through the dive. Once in the water we will get the President and make the switch with the clone. You will rescue the President from the diving mishap and he will be taken to the infirmary, where the good doctor will be ready to upload the President's memories with a couple of small alterations that will allow us to manipulate him. That's it."

"And what happens to me and the clone?"

"To you? You will be retired from service and

have the gratitude of your country. For the clone, he will take over your life."

Jess did not respond.

"Now, now Mr. Ehrlich don't be so glum. Enjoy your last few days."

Jess made an effort to get at Britin, but the restraints held him firmly in the chair. Britin did not react. He turned away and began to leave the room.

"Doctor. Let me know when you've finished. Have him taken back to his cell." Britin opened the door to the lab and left.

"Okay. Are you ready? Here we go." The doctor, who was standing in front of a large control panel a few feet away, began to start the process. He pushed some buttons and fine-tuned some dials.

Jess felt a sudden tingling behind his eyes. The implanted microchip felt warm in his forehead. There was no real pain, just a little discomfort. He tensed back into the chair and began to sweat profusely. He closed his eyes as the tingling grew and he began to feel like his head had been put in a vise that was beginning to squeeze tighter and tighter. He felt a numb headache swell forth. He tried to fight whatever was happening to him inside his head, but was helpless. He forced himself to fight whatever the thing in his forehead was doing to him.

"Mr. Ehrlich," the doctor who noticed Jess's

struggling called out. "There is nothing you can do to stop it. You will only make it harder on yourself. Just lie back and relax. It will all be over soon."

Jess heard but ignored the doctor. He continued to mentally block the microchip from its work. He began to shake under the strain. It was taking all of his strength. The doctor turned up a dial and increased the intensity of the procedure. It was too much for Jess to bear. Suddenly everything went black and he fell unconscious.

"You fool. I told you not to fight it." The doctor shook his head and continued to monitor the equipment.

Chapter 6

The restaurant was very quaint inside. It was decorated in the style of a restaurant that Monika went to on the Santa Barbara pier. She felt at home and had enjoyed the meal. As the waitress brought the bill, Monika decided to ask for directions to Jess's Dive Tours. She noted on the pamphlet that she held in her hand, that it was on Harbor lane.

"Excuse me," she politely addressed the waitress. "Can you tell me where Harbor Lane is?" Monika offered the waitress the pamphlet for further clarification.

"Oh. Jess's place. Yeah," she was chewing gum as she spoke. "His place isn't far from here. It's just down the street. Take the first right you come to. You can walk from here. It's only a couple of minutes."

"Thanks." Monika took back the pamphlet and the check from the waitress.

Putting her bag on the table, Monika took out her wallet and removed enough cash with a generous tip and placed it on top of the check on the table. She put the wallet back in her bag and got up from the table and left the restaurant. As she left, she noted the time on her wristwatch. It was 12:50 PM. There was still plenty of time to organize a trip out to the reef, but if it turned out that there wasn't, it didn't matter. She decided she would stay another day anyway before resuming her trip through the Keys.

When Monika left the restaurant the Corporal perked up. He watched as she stepped off the verandah. He expected her to go back to her car, but she didn't. She was heading in his direction. He ducked out of sight as she approached. He hoped she hadn't recognized him.

Monika walked down Seaside toward the ocean. It was a gorgeous day, sunny and warm. A little way down she spied a small gravel roadway going off to the right just before the beach. She came closer and read the signpost: Harbor Lane. She stopped a minute to take in the sight. Before her was a sandy cove and the vast azure blue ocean. There were several small sailing dinghies pulled up on the beach, their sails furled, waiting to be rented for the day. There were a dozen or so people on the beach and in the water. A Sea-doo with a spray of water shooting out of it into the air was speeding by, about fifty feet offshore.

Monika couldn't wait to join them. She continued on along Harbor Lane. About sixty feet ahead of her was a small beach shack. A small sign topped its black shingled roof: Jess's Dive Tours. This was the place. It was run down. An old sun-bleached Ford pick-up was parked to the left of the shack near the beach. There was scuba gear in the back. Beside it a Sea-doo, on its trailer, was parked. To the right of the shack were three large surfboards. The scene reminded her of a fifties 'Beach Party' movie. If he hadn't been recommended by Mrs. Lacure, Monika would have turned around and walked back to her car. But Mrs. Lacure had recommended him and Monika trusted her judgment. She continued on. There was no one in sight.

The Corporal waited several minutes before he carefully peeked out from his hiding. He had heard Monika's steps as she had walked by and wanted to be certain that she had moved farther along before he took up the chase. He saw her as she started down Harbor Lane. Quickly he got out of his car and started after her, making sure to keep out of sight.

"Hello? Anyone here." Monika had entered the shack. It was a small store space full of diving gear. There were tanks on the floor and regulators, fins, masks, wet suits and other equipment hanging on display on the walls. A small counter was directly in front of her about ten feet away. On the counter was an old cash register. Monika began to cross the showroom toward the counter.

"Hello? Is Jess Ehrlich here?" She stopped at the counter.

"At your service, ma'am," a voice emanated from behind the counter. "I'll be right with you."

"Okay." Monika was a little bewildered.

"Hi." A gorgeous blond-haired muscular man stood up from behind the counter. "Sorry about that. What can I do for you?" He was not wearing a top. He was very tanned and beachy looking. He was very amiable.

Monika was flabbergasted. This was the man from Pompano. The one who had drowned, but how could that be?

There was an awkward silence as Jess stood waiting for Monika's response, but there was none forthcoming.

Finally Jess repeated, "Ma'am? Can I help you?" He found this pretty woman odd.

"Oh I'm sorry. You look like someone I know. Have we met before?" It was a silly line, but Monika was shocked by Jess's similarity to the drowned man. "Do you have a brother?" Though she knew it was obviously a coincidence, the two men could have been identical twins.

"No." Jess thought this a strange question to ask. This woman acted as if she knew him, but he had never seen her before in his life. He decided to humor her and answered, "I'm an only child."

"Oh." Monika was still surprised, and now felt embarrassed by her behavior. "Sorry. It's just that you could be a twin."

"Sorry. I'm the only one." Jess smiled. "How can I help you?"

"I'm Monika Queller. Mrs. Lacure recommended you to me."

"Oh how is she? I haven't seen her in a while," Jess interrupted.

"She's fine. She said to say hi. She said you could show me the reef?"

"Sure can. When would you like to go?" Jess became friendlier now that the connection with Mrs. Lacure had been established.

"Is there time today?"

"Have you dived before?"

"Yes. I have my license. I've dived a lot in the Pacific, and some lake dives."

Jess checked the large diver's watch on his left wrist. "We could get a short dive in."

"Oh. I just had a light lunch." Monika didn't want to risk any problems in the water.

"That's all right. It will take us an hour to set-up and get to the dive site. You should be fine as long as it was a small lunch."

"I just had a sandwich."

"That'll be okay. Do you need gear?"

"Yes. Everything."

"We won't need a wet suit. The water's very warm here. So just tanks, fins, mask. Have you got your swim suit?"

"Yes." She had it on but wasn't going to tell him. "There's stuff in my car. I parked at Snapper's."

"Why don't you bring it over here and park next to the truck. I'll get the gear. Oh. What's your size."

"Five and a half."

"That's pretty small, but I think I have a pair of fins that will fit."

"Thanks. I'll be right back." Monika wasn't sure if Jess was complimenting or making fun of her. She turned and hurried out of the dive shop.

The Corporal was standing on Harbor Lane and was caught off-guard by Monika's sudden reappearance from the dive shop. He quickly turned and walked back up the lane trying to avoid contact with Monika. Twice in one day would be too much of a coincidence.

Monika noticed the Corporal as she came up the road. She was uncertain as to why he seemed familiar and though momentarily suspicious was in a hurry and did not give it much more conscious thought. Her unconscious mind, however, was mulling over both Jess's and now this man's familiarity to her. It was an oddity that she hadn't yet figured out.

By the time Monika returned to Jess's, Jess was standing out in front of the dive shop with all the gear, waiting for her.

"Hi. I think we have everything. You can leave your valuables and change in the shop. There's a change room inside. I'll start loading the boat." Jess pointed to a small white Chris Craft boat that was moored to the beach via a long rope. The rope was tethered to a concrete pylon that rose three feet from the sand fifteen feet from the waterline. The boat was three-quarters in the water and one quarter on the wet sand. Normally he kept it moored like this on shore, but on rough days and overnight he kept it anchored in the water just out of the surf.

"Thanks. I'll be right back." Monika went into the dive shop.

The Corporal was watching from the distance. He was not sure what he should do. It was clear that the girl was going out diving. He would not be able to follow. It was too risky. He decided to call in to his base and report. He took out his sat-phone and punched in a number. Placing the phone to his ear, he waited for an answer, keeping both Jess and the girl in sight.

"Britin," the ringing stopped and Major Britin answered.

"Sir. It's Corporal Vallins." He was formal when speaking to his superior officer.

"Go ahead Corporal. Report."

"The girl has met up with someone and is heading out to dive."

"Dive? Where are you?"

"Key Largo, Sir."

"Key Largo?"

"Yes Sir. She's at a Jess's Dive Tours."

"Jess's Dive Tours?! Are you certain?"

"Yes, Sir."

"Can you see who she's with?"

"Yes, Sir. It's a man. It looks like he's some sort of Dive Master."

"DIVE MASTER! Describe him."

"Young. Blond haired, physically fit."

There was silence on the other end of the phone. Major Britin had not expected this from this girl. Maybe it wasn't a coincidence at the beach in Pompano. He chided himself for not doing a more thorough background check on her.

"Bring her in, Corporal." Britin would play it safe and bring her to the base in Key West. There he could keep her under lock and key until the mission was finished. He did not want to risk the mission. He would get a complete background check on her by the time she arrived. She may not be a threat, but he couldn't risk it.

"Yes, Sir. But she's going out with him in a boat. Should I get them both?"

"No," Britin was firm. He did not want the clone disturbed or threatened, and he did not want to let the Corporal have any idea who the Dive Master really was. "Stay where you are."

"Sir?"

"Wait 'til she comes back and is alone. I don't want any witnesses. Understand Corporal Vallins?" There was a threatening tone in Britin's voice. It was clear what he expected and that he would not tolerate any mistakes.

"Yes Sir." The Corporal understood his orders.

"Do not. I repeat. Do not harm the Dive Master, under any circumstances."

"Understood, Sir." The Corporal heard the line disconnect as he uttered his acknowledgment. He breathed a sigh of relief. Major Britin was a hard man and he did not want to do anything that would upset him.

Resigned to spending the day waiting at the beach, the Corporal put the phone away. He watched as the boat that carried Jess and Monika gradually motored farther and farther out into the ocean. He hoped they would return soon. He wanted to get out of this heat and sun.

- - - - - - - - - - - - - -

The noise of the engine drowned out all other sound. The boat rose up and down as it made its way through the gentle swells of the ocean. Jess's dive shop was now far away on shore.

The trip was exhilarating. Spray from the water occasionally found its way into the boat and struck her as they bounced over the water. The speed of the boat created a refreshing breeze. They did not speak as they traveled, but Jess made an occasional check on Monika and smiled.

It was not long before Jess began to slow the motor and they arrived at the dive site. Over the side the coral reef could be seen not far below. The water was clean and clear, and the twisting shapes and colors of the reef easily seen.

"See the anchor in the back?" Jess could be easily heard. The motor was quietly running in neutral.

"Yes." Monika saw a small sea anchor attached to a heavy rope which was cleated to the boat. She went over to it and picked it up. It was heavy, but she managed to lift and hold it.

"When I say, throw it over the side."

"Okay." She struggled a bit with the anchor.

Jess maneuvered the boat slowly and shut off the motor. "Okay. Drop it."

Monika threw the anchor over the starboard side of the boat. It made a loud splash and sank below the surface. The rope it was attached to rapidly followed after it and unfurled. Within a few seconds the downward journey of the rope stopped. The anchor had touched bottom.

"That's great." Jess was getting out of the driver's seat and came back into the open area of the boat where Monika and all the dive gear were waiting. "We'll dive here. It's a protected area and we won't have to worry about sharks or barracuda. It's shallow here."

"Sharks and barracuda?" Monika didn't like the sound of these man-eaters.

"Don't worry. They really aren't a problem in these waters, but you have to be careful. The reefs are a feeding ground for them, but that's usually at night or in the early morning. This place here has never had a sighting. That's why I come here. We'll be fine." Jess was getting ready. "Do you need any help? That's your gear." He pointed to a neat pile of scuba equipment.

"No I'm fine." Monika knew what to do. The realization that there might be danger lurking below had sobered her for a moment.

After several minutes, both Jess and Monika had entered into the water by somersaulting backwards over the stern of the boat and bobbing in the water. Jess took his breather out of his mouth.

"Keep close to me. If there's a problem, do this." He made a hand sign for Monika to see.

"Okay." Monika tried to say through her mouthpiece as she also nodded her acknowledgment. Her voice was muffled and not very audible.

Jess put his mouthpiece back and signaled that they should both dive. Monika gave a thumbs-up and they submerged below the water.

The moment that Monika became immersed in the water, she entered a whole new world. The water was warm and encapsulating. There was a complete silence other than the sound of her breathing through the regulator and the bubbling of the exhaled air through the water as it tried to find its way back to the world a few short feet above. She became very aware of herself and her belonging to that world. She was only a visitor here—a visitor that was bound by strict limitations.

The water here was not very deep. She could have made the dive with only snorkeling equipment, but the scuba gear allowed her to really become a part of this submariner world. The ocean floor consisted of clean white sand. As far as the eye could see there were all sorts of varieties of coral and reef plant-life. Yellows, greens, reds, whites, pinks, purples, every color imaginable was here. It was a breath-taking experience. An occasional fish darted between the coral as both she and Jess approached. They swam deeper into the reef, Jess in the lead and Monika back behind to his left. She wished she had brought an underwater camera to capture the sight, but realized that she would definitely return tomorrow and could take pictures then.

Shortly they swam off the shallow reef and entered into deeper water. The reflection from the sky above turned the water into a brilliant azure blue, Monika's favorite color. Jess stopped in the water and got Monika's attention. He was pointing out something ahead and coming their way. Monika followed his pointing and beheld a magnificent sight. A school of Porkfish and Grunts was approaching and not at all spooked by their presence. The yellow and black striped Porkfish were the most numerous, but were interspersed with the more plain white grunt.

She and Jess continued swimming and soon found themselves amongst them. Monika, though excited, was a little perturbed by them occasionally rubbing against her, but soon got used to the phenomenon. She giggled through her mouthpiece. The fish seemed unafraid of her intrusion to their school, greeting her and Jess with interest and curiosity. Monika was impressed that they were so tame. She carefully swam through the water and followed Jess who was leading her to another part of the reef.

Several lengths away the school of fish had passed by. Jess had stopped by a large three foot diameter coral ball. It looked like a large human brain. He beckoned her over. At the ball there were several small fish hovering. Monika slowly swam up to Jess and the fish. Jess moved his hand carefully over to one of the fish, as if he was going to pat a dog. The fish moved an inch or so away. Jess stopped. He looked at Monika through his mask and communicated with his eyes that she should try. Monika nodded and cautiously pushed her hand towards the fish. As with Jess's attempt, the fish moved about an inch away from her hand and stopped. He hovered in place above the coral ball and, with his large unblinking eyes, observed Monika through her goggles. Their eyes met. It was a great thrill.

Jess communicated by hand and facial gestures that she should spend some time and explore this part of the reef. Monika understood and left Jess to explore this area of the reef. To her amazement the little fish that she had attempted to pat began to follow her. Monika smiled to herself and turned to see the fish. She muttered a hello through her mouthpiece. The fish was frightened by the sound of the bubbling water that resulted from the greeting and darted away.

There were lots of sights to be seen. The longer she remained here in this world, the more she became an accepted part of it. As she swam she noted that many more fish were swimming around her and now totally unconcerned about her presence as they continued foraging for food amongst the coral.

The time flew by and before long, Monika felt the touch of Jess's hand upon her left arm. Jess looked at Monika through her goggles and, once he had her attention, brought his wristwatch in front of her and tapped it with his other hand and then pointed up. It was time to surface. Monika didn't want to leave but she nodded her head and followed Jess back through the water to the place where they had set off from.

As they broke the surface, they removed their

mouthpieces and bobbed in the water at the stern of the boat. The sound of the waves breaking against the boat, the clean fresh ocean air and the warmth of the sun on her face, reminded Monika on a sensual level that she had returned to her world.

"That was unbelievable," she gasped, short of breath. "How long were we down there?"

"Almost an hour." Jess was comfortable in the water and was showing no strain from treading water.

"Wow. That long. It only seemed like ten minutes."

"It's always like that."

"The fish were so friendly."

"Yeah. This part of the reef doesn't get a lot of tourists and they haven't learnt to fear us yet."

"Can we do this again tomorrow?"

"Yeah, but only tomorrow. I'm going to Key West on Wednesday for a few days."

- - - - - - - - - - - - - - -

It had been a long hot afternoon. Corporal Vallins had removed his shoes and socks, and rolled up his shirtsleeves. He had dark navy issue sunglasses on, but had neglected to bring a hat. His face was pink from sunburning.

After Monika had set out on the boat, Vallins had returned to his car and driven it down Seaside past Harbor to where it ended at the beach. There was a small parking lot right at the ocean. He parked under a couple of tall date palm trees, opened all the windows and turned the engine off. From here he had a clear view and would be able to see Monika's return. He got out of the car and went back up the street to Snappers and got a take-out lunch and a coffee. He then hurried back to the car, though he felt certain they would not have returned in the few minutes it took him to make his lunch trip. He got back into the car and looked over the beach out into the ocean.

As he sat waiting he tried to plan when and where he would abduct the girl. He had some chloroform with him that he would use, but he required an opportunity to use it. He thought it would be best to wait 'til it was dark and then make his move. He hoped that she was going to stay nearby and not travel back to Pompano for the night. It would be harder to get to her in Pompano.

Out of the blue horizon came the boat heading for shore. Corporal Vallins put his binoculars to his eyes and, bringing them into focus, clearly made out both Jess and Monika. They seemed happy. The Corporal was relieved that it was them. Several similar boats had sailed by during the afternoon, which had taken him from resting to active duty, but they had all been false alarms. This time he took the glasses away from his eyes and checked his wristwatch and grinned. It was just after 4:30 PM. It had not been as long as he had expected.

- - - - - - - - - - - - - - -

Jess revved up the engines and then shut them off as the boat came within the last few feet of surf. This final surge pushed the boat forward as it rode a wave and embedded itself about three feet onto the wet sand of the beach. He jumped from his driver's seat and hopped over the side, taking with him a long rope that was cleated to the front of the boat.

"Hold on. I'll pull us farther up," he shouted.

"Okay," Monika acknowledged.

Jess went to the front of the boat and waited for the next cresting wave and then heaved the boat forward. It moved a couple of feet. The boat was now firmly settled on shore.

"Okay," he called out to let Monika know she could now get out.

Monika carefully made her way as far forward as she could before lifting herself over the side into the shallow surf. She had had a great day. Having nothing to carry, she made her way up the beach. The sand was warm against her bare feet. It felt good.

Jess had gone ahead and was tying the rope from the boat to the pylon in the beach in front of his shop. Monika got to him just as he was finishing.

"Thank you. That was the best." Monika truly had had a great time.

"You're welcome." Jess finished tying and stood up.

"Would you like me to settle up now, or tomorrow?"

"Tomorrow's fine." Jess trusted Monika —he prided himself at being a good judge of people.

"What time's good?" Monika sounded like an excited schoolgirl.

"How about eleven?"

"Sounds great."

"Are you staying locally tonight?"

"Yes. At the Sandy Cove Resort. If they have a room."

"They should. Tell them I sent you over, and ask for cabin eight. It's the nicest, secluded, and right on the beach. You'll love it." He was being helpful. She was cute, nice, and deserved it. He couldn't help but think what a lucky guy her fiancé was to have her. He would die for someone like her.

"Thank you. I'll get my stuff."

"Go ahead. I've got to get the gear."

"See you tomorrow."

"Okay. Bye."

Monika went up the beach and into the dive shop. It wasn't locked. She was not surprised. It seemed like the type of place where you didn't have to worry about such things.

- - - - - - - - - - - - - -

The Corporal, having witnessed the interchange on the beach, watched as Monika went into the dive shop and within a few minutes came out with her things. The shop was in clear view from his parked location. She went over to her car, threw everything into the back, got in and then started back up Harbor Lane to Seaside. He crouched low in his car as she turned left heading to Highway 1. When she had gone up Seaside a little farther, he started his car and began to follow her.

- - - - - - - - - - - - - - -

The Sandy Reef Resort was five minutes away and right on Highway 1. Monika saw the sign and pulled onto the side street that led the two hundred yards into its main entry. It was a cute place in the style of a thirties camp, nestled into a little cove right on the ocean. It was beautifully kept and welcoming. She parked in a spot under a large palm tree, got her things and went into the main office area.

"Good afternoon," she was greeted by a young man just inside the doorway.

"Hi." Monika was caught off-guard by this pleasantry.

"Are you checking-in?"

"Yes." She suddenly realized that the young man was the doorman.

"Over there to your right, ma'am. Welcome to the Sandy Reef," he indicated a small countered area about fifteen feet away. A woman was busy behind the counter.

"Thank you." Monika crossed to the counter.

The room was nicely decorated in off-whites and pastel colors. There were lovely watercolors on the walls and the furnishings were casual and beachy. It had the feel of an expensive five star resort but she did not care, she was on vacation and was going to spoil herself.

"Hi," she said as she came to the woman at the counter and put her large bag on the floor beside her. "Can I get a room for the night?"

"Yes ma'am. Just for you?" The woman was in her early forties, heavy set with short red hair and glasses that were out of style.

"Yes. Jess sent me."

"Oh, Jess. How's he doing? I haven't seen him in a while. He's been acting strange lately."

"He seems fine. He said to ask for cabin eight. Is it available?"

The woman typed something onto a keyboard in front of her and regarded the small computer screen that was built into and flush with her desktop area behind the countertop. "Yes. How many nights?" she asked, not looking up.

"Just tonight. I'm heading through the Keys tomorrow."

"That'll be a nice trip. We're having great weather. Can I have your name?"

"Monika Queller."

"And what is your home address Ms. Queller?"

"1625 Garden Lane, Santa Barbara, 94301."

"Do you want the key to the mini-bar?"

"No thanks."

"How will you be paying."

"Credit card."

"May I have the card please?"

Monika put her handbag on the counter, removed her wallet, found her credit card and handed it to the woman.

"Thank you." She took the card and ran it through her system. She waited and watched the screen.

"Okay." The woman left her terminal and from the wall behind her picked a set of keys. "You're in cabin eight. Joel here," she indicated the young doorman, who she also beckoned over, "will help you."

"Thank you." Monika took the key.

"Oh, Here's your card. Sorry." The woman handed Monika the validated credit card, which Monika put back into her wallet and then her handbag.

"Joel," she said to the doorman who was now at the counter behind Monika. "Show Ms. Queller to cabin eight."

"Yes ma'am." Joel picked up Monika's bag from the floor. "Is this everything ma'am?" he asked.

"No. There's some luggage in my car."

"I'll show you to your room ma'am, and then if you give me your car keys, I'll park your car in front of your cabin and get your other luggage to you shortly."

"That'll be fine. There's no hurry." Monika took the rental car keys from her handbag and handed them over. "It's the small white one." There was a license number on the key chain.

"Thank you. Follow me please."

"Have a nice stay," the woman at the counter added.

"Thank you, I will." Monika responded and then turned to follow the doorman. "What a lovely spot," she thought.

Joel led Monika out from the main office along a curving interlocking yellow brick pathway to a cute cabin about a hundred feet from the main office. The sandy Reef was comprised of several small cabins and a main complex, which contained most of the guestrooms. Cabin eight, which looked like a dollhouse, was by far the most favorably placed of all the cabins that Monika could see. It was inches from the beach and faced out over the ocean.

"Here you are ma'am." Joel, using Monika's keys, opened the door. Monika went in, Joel followed.

The inside of the cabin was larger than Monika expected. Decorated in modern off-whites, there was a main room with a cream-colored fabric couch, a glass table in front of it, white sheer drapes and modern art deco lamps and windows that overlooked the beach and ocean. It was breathtaking. There was a closed door to the right of the couch. She wondered if it led to the bedroom.

"Your room and bath are in there," Joel, as if on cue, offered. "If you need anything, just let me know." He put the bag down and waited.

Monika understood. She took some loose change out of her bag and handed it to him.

"Thank you."

"Thank you ma'am. If it's okay, The rest of your luggage will be brought to you shortly."

"That's okay. I don't need anything right away. I'm just going to sit and relax."

"Thank you, ma'am. Have a nice stay." The doorman turned and left the room.

- - - - - - - - - - - - - - - -

Corporal Vallins had been watching Monika's every move. He was pleased with her choice of the cabin. It would make his job easy. As soon as it was dark he would drive over to the cabin and get the girl. By late tonight she would be secured in the Key West Naval base jail. His mission would be accomplished.

- - - - - - - - - - - - - - - -

Monika awoke to the sound of knocking at her cabin door. Her watch read 8:20 PM. She had fallen asleep on the couch. She quickly rose and answered the door.

"Sorry to disturb you ma'am." It was the doorman. "I tried earlier but you didn't answer. I thought you might want your things before it got too late."

"Oh. Of course. I fell asleep. Thank you for waking me." She stood aside and Joel brought in her other bags.

"Where would you like them, ma'am?"

"That's fine there. I'll get them later."

"Yes ma'am." He placed the luggage in the room beside the couch. "Will there be anything else?" he asked as he returned Monika's car keys.

"No. Thank you." Monika took the keys and handed him a good tip.

"Thank you." Joel, pleased, turned and shut the door behind him as he left.

Monika considered if she should unpack right away and then go and get some dinner, or if she should wait and stay in and order from room service. She decided to stay in. She could freshen up while she waited for room service to deliver. She crossed to the table in front of the couch and picked up the phone and pushed the Room Service button. The phone rang at the other end.

"Room Service."

"Hi. This is cabin eight. What's the dinner special?" Monika listened as the person in room service described the meal.

"That sounds good. Could you send it over in half an hour?"

There was a short answer.

"Thank you." Monika hung up. She had plenty

of time to freshen-up.

She lifted one of her suitcases onto the couch and opened it. She took out her toiletry bag. Noticing that it was getting dark, she went to the window to pull the drapes. There was a marvelous sun setting before her. Reds, blues, violet, all sorts of colors could be seen as the sinking sun reflected into the rippling ocean before her. Jess had been correct. This was a fabulous cabin. She closed the drapes and headed for the bathroom to take a shower.

- - - - - - - - - - - - - - -

Corporal Vallins had seen the doorman leave and was considering when he should make his move. It was getting dark, and there wasn't anyone around the cabin. He waited about ten minutes and, seeing no one in the vicinity, decided that now was the time. He started his car, put on his lights and slowly drove over to and parked in front of the cabin. He turned the lights out, but left the car running. He waited a few moments inside the car as he readied himself. He wanted the abduction to be accomplished quickly and without any undo attention. He took out the small bottle of chloroform and gauze from the glove compartment, undid the cap and soaked the gauze. He held his breath, not wanting to be affected by the drug.

Getting out from the car, he surveyed the area. The coast was still clear. He made his move. He went up to the cabin door and loudly knocked.

- - - - - - - - - - - - - - -

Monika had just gotten into the warm shower when she heard a loud pounding at her door. She was aggravated by it. She wondered who it might be. Room Service wasn't due for a while.

Turning off the water, she got out from the shower, picked up a fluffy white towel and held it to her chest. She came out of the bathroom and into the main room. She was not pleased that the knocking had interrupted her shower.

"Who is it?" Monika asked angrily.

The knocking stopped. There was a pause and then, "Room Service," came back through the door.

"You're early. I told you in half an hour." Monika complained.

"Sorry ma'am."

"Oh all right. Just a minute." There was nothing that she could do about it now, but she was going to call the resort manager and complain. She didn't understand how the meal had been prepared so fast.

Being in a hurry, Monika dropped the towel bent over, and quickly took out her jeans and her Stanford gray sweatshirt from the open suitcase on the couch and put them on.

"I'll be right there," she announced as she hurriedly pulled the clothes on.

She tousled her hair, which fortunately was not

wet and went over to the door. She undid the lock
and was about to turn the handle when the door
was brutally thrown open. Monika was pushed
back and about to complain when a large man was
upon her and holding a chloroformed gauze over
her nose and mouth.

Monika screamed and struggled, but the scream
was muffled by the gauze and the man was too
strong to get away from. He had a firm grip on
her. She inhaled the drug and realized what was
happening. She tried not to breath, but the effort
of her fighting forced her to inhale more of the
drug.

She continued to fight with all her might. Their
eyes met. Suddenly she recognized her attacker as
the man from the coffee shop in Ft. Lauderdale
this morning and on the road by the restaurant at
lunch. She tried to murmur some words through
the gauze at the Corporal, but was beginning to
feel the effects of the drug as it found its way into
her system and numbed her. The drug had a bittersweet taste. Slowly her struggle diminished
and within seconds of the Corporal's forced entry
and smothering, she fell unwillingly unconscious.

The Corporal held onto Monika firmly as she
went limp in his arms. He waited a few more
moments before removing the chloroform soaked
gauze from her face. Satisfied that she was
knocked out, he picked her up in his arms as if she
were weightless, and went out through the door.

As he left, he pulled the door handle with his left
elbow and closed it. An open door would draw
unwanted interest that might hinder his escape.
His adrenaline was pumping as he reconnoitered
the area to see if the struggle with Monika had
been heard. There was no one in sight. He crossed
to his car. He opened the back door and placed
Monika on the seat. Quickly he went to his door,
opened it and got in behind the wheel. After closing the door, he turned on his lights and backed
away from the cabin. When he had enough room
he put the car in drive and drove off down the
roadway. He started so rapidly that the car's rear
wheels squealed but he didn't care, he felt safe.
He drove up the roadway and signaled to turn
onto Highway 1 heading south for Key West.
Within two hours he would be at the base. No one
at the resort would know what happened. Monika
would remain asleep until he arrived in Key West.
He had given her a large dose of the drug. The
Corporal smiled. It was a clean get-away.

- - - - - - - - - - - - - - -

"It's Room Service."

A young woman with a tray full of covered
plates was standing in front of cabin eight waiting
for a reply. She had been there several minutes
and there had been no reply to her repeated
knocking. She was new on staff at the Sandy Reef
and didn't want any problems.

"Hello? Ms. Queller. Room Service?" she again

knocked and called out.

She waited a few more minutes and decided to leave the tray on the threshold. Maybe the guest was in the middle of something and didn't want to be disturbed. Bending down she placed the heavy tray in front of the door and then left to return to her other duties. She would return later during her night shift to retrieve the tray. She was annoyed that she had not been given a tip, but hoped that the guest would leave one on the chit after she had finished her meal.

Chapter 7

Eleven o'clock had come and gone. Jess, ready at the dive shop, was wondering what was keeping Monika. It was a perfect day for the dive. The ocean was calm and the day was already hot and sunny. Not a cloud was in the sky. He had not expected Monika to be late. She had seemed a very reliable and honest person. He hoped that he hadn't been stiffed for yesterday's dive.

At eleven forty-five, having still not seen her, he went into his shop and picked up the phone. He dialed the Sandy Reef Resort.

"Sandy Reef Resort. Good morning," a woman cheerfully answered the phone.

"Hi. Is that Margaret?" Jess inquired having

recognized the voice.

"Yes. Speaking." Margaret had not yet recognized Jess's voice.

"Margaret. It's Jess. Jess Ehrlich."

"Oh. Hi Jess. How are you?" Margaret was pleased to hear from him. "We haven't seen you in a while. Where have you been?"

"I've been away a couple of weekends on reserve duty." He wasn't allowed to mention that he was involved in the upcoming President's visit and that he had spent a couple of weekends away being briefed and prepared for his part in the visit. "You know how it is. The time flies by."

"Well don't let it go too long. You still owe me a drink," she was toying with him.

"I haven't forgotten, but that's not why I'm calling." He abruptly changed the subject.

"How can I help you?" Margaret, sensing the change in tone, became business-like.

"Did a Monika Queller register last night?"

"Just a minute I'll check the computer. That's Queller?"

"Yes I think so."

Margaret typed the name into the computer database. In seconds Monika's name popped up on the screen.

"Yes. She's in cabin eight." Margaret became curious, "A new friend?" She wondered if this was a girlfriend of his.

"No nothing like that." Jess understood

Margaret's question. "She was meant to be here at eleven for a dive, but she hasn't shown up."

"Well she hasn't checked out. Maybe she's slept in. Would you like me to put you through to her room?

"Please."

"And Jess," Margaret added before she connected him. "Come by and see me soon."

"I will. Thanks." Jess held the receiver to his ear as Margaret transferred his call to Monika's room.

The phone rang and rang. After six or seven rings it was answered.

"Sandy Reef Resort. Good morning." It was Margaret again. The unanswered call had bounced back to the front desk.

"Hi Margaret. It's me again. There was no answer." Jess was agitated.

"I can take a message if you'd like and give it to her when I see her."

"Okay. Tell her I called about the dive."

"I will."

"Thanks."

"You're welcome Jess." Margaret hung up.

Jess was bothered that there had been no answer. Monika had seemed so excited about today's dive. Maybe she was en route and something had happened. He decided to wait another half-hour before putting the gear away. Maybe she would still show up.

- - - - - - - - - - - - - - -

Monika awakened to find herself sitting in a chair in front of a four legged cheap metal table in a small dirty room. There was a dirty light in a cage in the ceiling. There were no windows in the room and the walls were painted a drab gray. She was a little groggy and felt like she had a bad hangover. Her head ached.

"Ms. Queller. Nice to have you with us." It was Major Britin. He was seated in front of her on the other side of the table. Behind him, standing in front of a door that was the only exit to the room, was Corporal Vallins.

"Who are you? What's going on? Where am I?" Monika blurted out questions. She was afraid and cold. Recognizing the Corporal sobered her. She remembered the struggle in her room and the chemical smell over her nose and mouth.

"Slow down Ms. Queller. We'll get to all of that. I'm Major Britin. I'm in charge of this base."

"What base? Why have you kidnapped me?"

"You're in Key West, and we haven't kidnapped you, but we do need the answers to a few questions."

"What questions?" The floor was cold on her bare feet so she lifted them onto the chair leg supports.

"Corporal. Get Ms. Queller something for her feet." He noted her discomfort.

"Yes Sir." The Corporal turned, opened the door and left the room.

"Sorry we had to bring you here so unannounced, but it was a national security issue."

"I don't understand." Monika was lost.

"The President is arriving in Ft. Jefferson on Friday."

"So what has that got to do with me. Why have you brought me here?" she pleaded.

"Your boyfriend, a James Anstey, works for the CIA in Los Angeles?" The Major ignored her questions and followed his own agenda.

"How do you know that?"

"It's all here in this report." The Major was reading from a piece of paper that he had taken out of a file folder that was on the desk in front of him.

"Report?"

"We've done a check on you. You've got quite an interesting background."

"What do you want? What's going on?" Monika still wasn't following him and she was so tired. She wanted to get out of here. Every part of her was telling her to escape. To get away. That this Major wasn't what he said he was. Her guard was very high.

"That's what I would like to know. Why were you with Jess Ehrlich?"

"Who?"

"Jess's Dive Tours?"

"Oh. That Jess." Monika made the connection. Somehow this involved Jess. So that's what this was about. Maybe Jess was a spy or something. "What do you mean?"

"Now Ms. Queller. Don't play games with me. This can go easy or hard," his tone roughened as he gave her a menacing glare.

"What are you talking about? I'm here on vacation to meet James' family." She was getting more desperate.

"Who are you working for? CIA? FBI? Why are you really meeting this James Anstey? Who are you really? You aren't fooling anyone." Britin was direct. He was beginning to apply pressure.

"Are you nuts? You've got me confused with someone else. I want out of here. Now!" Monika was angry and scared. She screamed out her words.

"Until you cooperate, Ms. Queller. You will remain here 'til after the President's visit. We can't take any chances."

"I am cooperating. You have no right…" Monika was interrupted by a knock at the door and the Corporal's re-entry. He was carrying a small pair of Navy issue running shoes.

"Corporal. Good. You found something. Give them to Ms. Queller and then take her downstairs."

"Yes Sir." The Corporal put the shoes on the table in front of her.

"I'm not going anywhere. I want a lawyer." Monika crossed her arms in front of her.

"One way or another you will do as you're told. Now the Corporal here can do it the easy way or the hard way. It's up to you. Until we check out your story, you're going to remain here, in protective custody. As long as the President's security is involved, I can do whatever I like."

"But I'm not here to do anything to the President. You've made a mistake."

"Well then, you have nothing to worry about. It will all be over Friday. Until then, and until we can check your story, you are under military arrest and will remain here."

Monika was not sure what she could do. Her emotions were all jumbled. She felt like crying, but wasn't going to react the way the Major probably expected her to. She would remain alert and strong. There was nothing she could do at this moment, but she would look for an opportunity. She had no choice but to cooperate.

"Good. I see you understand. You are a smart woman." Getting no response or complaint the Major took Monika's silence as acceptance of his terms. "Now, put on your shoes and go with the Corporal." His tone was comforting and commanding, like a stern parent.

Monika picked the running shoes off the table. They were heavy. She bent down and put them on her feet. It was nice to protect them from the cold hard floor. As she bent below the table she saw a three inch loose piece of thin cylindrical metal on the floor by her foot and the table leg. It must have been a part of the leg support to the table. She carefully slipped it into her shoe as she tied the laces. She wasn't sure what good it would do, but she took it anyway. Neither of the two men noticed. She stood up. The Corporal took her arm and guided her past the Major and through the door into a hallway. Nothing was said.

The hallway was narrow and also painted the same drab gray color. There were no windows or doors. It was just a hallway. There was a single row of six caged yellowing lights situated centrally along the ceiling. Some of the lights had burnt out and others were flickering. The Corporal had a strong grip on her arm and was pushing her forward along the hall.

"Hey," Monika complained. "You're hurting me. Not so hard."

He ignored her and continued to hold her firmly. He was under orders not to converse with the prisoner.

"Where are we going? You guys have made a mistake. Your leader there is nuts."

The Corporal gave no indication of hearing her.

"Oh you don't talk." Monika realized that she would not get any answers from him.

They walked down the hall and came to a stairwell. The stairwell was old and dirty. It was dimly lit by another yellowing caged light that protruded from the wall about ten steps down on a small landing where another set of zig zagging stairs continued down.

They both went down the stairs about, as far as she could determine, two floors and came to a steel door. It was locked. The Corporal took out a set of keys, unlocked it, opened it and pushed Monika roughly into another corridor. At this level there was a damp stench and the air was cooler. She felt the skin along her arms, neck and chest rise in goosebumps. Her nipples, which were brushing against the soft cotton of her sweatshirt, hardened. This was the brig. Monika was afraid of this dark place. She stood still in the corridor. It was claustrophobic. Though it had the same layout as the hallway above, it was much more dirty and dank. Only a couple of the caged ceiling lights were working. The air was stale. It reminded her of a dungeon.

The Corporal shoved her forward. She shuffled her upper body against his hold in protest to his roughness, and reluctantly continued.

- - - - - - - - - - - - - - -

From inside his cell, Jess heard the footsteps coming down the corridor. He was awake and determined this time to put up a fight with the soldiers. He had had enough of this imprisonment and had nothing left to lose. It was very clear to him that he was not going to be allowed out of here alive. The stakes were high.

The footsteps became louder as they

approached his cell and then stopped. Jess threw himself tightly into the corner of his cell on top of his bed farthest away from the door and braced himself. He readied himself to pounce like a mountain lion upon whoever entered. It would be his one last valiant struggle.

He waited, all tensed. He heard a key placed in the door lock and twisted, but to his surprise it was not his cell door that was being unlocked rather, the one directly opposite him. It suddenly dawned upon him that someone else was being brought into the brig as a prisoner. He intently listened to every sound, his mind spinning with curiosity. He heard the other cell door creak open and the sound of someone being pushed in. Then the creak of the door as it closed and the twisting sound of the key in the lock, followed by the clank of the door locking mechanism falling into position.

He fully expected his own cell door to be unlocked next and readied himself again for the attack. But nothing happened. The sound of the footsteps going back up the corridor resumed. They become fainter and fainter, until finally there was no more trace of them. Jess was bewildered. He wondered who could be in the other cell?

- - - - - - - - - - - - - - -

Monika was now sitting in her cell on the metal bed. The drug had completely worn off. She had a sharp pain in her abdomen. She pulled up her sweatshirt and examined the area around her belly button. She found a tiny scab. It was the size of a pinprick and sore. She didn't remember how it had happened. She began to weep. She had gone as far as her emotions would allow her. The ordeal of her interrogation was behind her. She was now a prisoner in an unknown place, by unknown captors. No one knew where she was and no one would be able to help her. She wondered why this was happening to her. What had she done? She didn't like this place. It was cold, damp and uncomforting. She felt disoriented and afraid. Her tears swelled forth. She began to weep. She lay down on the uncomfortable bed and fell asleep.

- - - - - - - - - - - - - - -

"Hi Margaret." Jess had waited before calling the Sandy Reef. It was now after lunch and he wanted to settle up any loose ends before he started for Key West in the morning. He was supposed to report to the old Naval base and from there he was to be shipped over to Ft. Jefferson. He would have all Thursday to prepare, check the diving gear and have a couple of run-throughs of the dive before the President arrived on Friday. He was looking forward to the honor of guiding the President, and didn't need the aggravation of being stiffed by a client hovering over him.

"Hi Jess."

"Did Ms. Queller get my message? I haven't heard or seen her."

"No. In fact, she's not here."

"What? When did she check out?"

"She hasn't checked out. She's just not here. Room Service reported that she didn't answer her door last night and the meal was untouched. Her car is parked out front of her cabin."

"Maybe she skipped out on the rental car as well."

"No. Housekeeping found all her luggage still unpacked in her room. There's something wrong. The resort has called the authorities. There might be foul play involved."

"What? I don't believe it. Was there any struggle?'

"No nothing. It's as if she was interrupted in the middle of things. There's no sign of struggle or break-in. It's a mystery. She's just vanished." It was clear from Margaret's voice that she was both concerned for Monika's plight, but also thrilled that such an occurrence could happen here in quiet Key Largo.

"Well. Let me know when she turns up. She's probably out shopping or something." Though it was unusual, Jess did not believe that anything untoward had happened to Monika.

"I will."

"I'm out of town 'til Saturday, so you won't be able to reach me, but I'll check my messages."

"Okay. Have a nice trip."

"Thanks. I hope everything turns out okay. Bye."

"Bye."

Jess hung up his phone and pondered what Margaret had told him. It was very odd.

- - - - - - - - - - - - - - - -

Lunch was brought late that day to the prisoners and consisted of beans and corn bread and a cup of water. Jess had been considering all that morning whether or not he should attempt to communicate with the other prisoner, but had decided to wait. Other than the sobbing he had heard from her cell earlier in the night, he had heard nothing. He was amazed that it was apparently a female prisoner opposite him. He also considered that it might be some sort of trick to try and get to him, though he wasn't sure why such a game would be played he was going to be cautious. After lunch had been delivered and the soldier who had brought it left, he went to his cell door and listened. He heard no sounds.

He waited until he was certain there was no one else in the corridor before he spoke out. He carefully peered through his tiny barred window into the corridor. He strained his head to try and see up and down the corridor. He took his left arm, placed it through the window and tried, using the dim reflection in his wristwatch crystal, to see more. He could see no one. Satisfied that the corridor was empty, he decided to make his next step.

"Hey. You. In the cell," he called out in a loud whisper. "Over here."

Monika was lying on her bed. She was thinking about James. She missed him and wished there was a way to let him know what was happening.

"Hey. You over there. Psst. Psst." Jess tried a little louder.

Monika thought she heard something. She focused her attention. She wasn't sure if it was just this place and her mind playing tricks on her. She had seen so many movies with a scene like this that she didn't trust her senses.

"Psst. Over here."

She rose up from her bed. The sound was coming from outside her cell. It was the whispered voice of a man. The voice seemed familiar. Monika became intrigued.

"Psst. Psst," came louder.

She carefully peered through her barred window. The corridor was dimly lit.

"Psst. Over here." Jess could make out Monika's startling blue eyes, tiny nose and blond hair.

She looked out and found the source of the voice. It was a male prisoner in the cell opposite hers. She could not see him very well.

"Hi," Jess began. He brought his right index finger to his lips to indicate that they should speak quietly so as not to alert their captors. "Are you okay?"

Monika was stunned. She couldn't believe that this was happening. "Yes," she nodded as she spoke, being careful not to be too loud.

"I'm Jesse." Jess used his proper name with his more intimate friends and family. In this situation it seemed more natural for him.

"Monika," she replied. "Where are we?"

"We're in the old abandoned Naval Base in Key West. In the lower level brig."

"How long have you been here?"

"A few weeks. I'm not sure."

"Where are you from?"

"California. I'm here on vacation for a couple of weeks."

Jesse wondered why they would be interested in Monika. "What do you do?"

"I teach high school."

"Why did they bring you here?"

"I don't know. I was being followed from Pompano Beach to Key Largo. Some guy knocked at my door and put something on my face and I passed out. Next thing I know I'm here being interrogated by that Major guy."

"What were you doing in Key Largo?"

"I was diving the coral reef."

Jesse thought for a minute. It all seemed so innocent. Out of professional curiosity he wondered who Monika had used as a guide. "Which dive company did you use?"

Monika thought this was a strange question, but answered anyway. "Jess's Dive Tours. He's a nice guy,"

Jesse stepped back from his window in shock. So what Britin had told him was true. They had managed to clone him and use their new technology to upload all his memory to make a perfect duplicate.

"Jesse?" Monika had expected a reply. Not getting any she called out. "You know," she continued, "It's odd that you have a similar name." She was more comfortable and her mind was beginning to note the coincidence. This trip had had so many coincidences. She waited for his answer, but there was none. "Jesse?"

Oh. Sorry." Jesse was jarred back from his thoughts.

"Do you know him?" she asked as she saw him come closer to his window. She saw him better now and was trying to figure out why he was so familiar. There was something about his voice and look.

"Yes. Very well."

"Really."

"It's me," he gave her a stare through the windows. Their eyes met. "I'm Jesse Ehrlich."

"What?!" It was incredulous. "How? That's not possible. You're up in Key Largo."

"No I'm here, and have been for weeks."

The voice was definitely Jess's. But Monika

knew that was not possible. Jess had no brothers. Maybe this was a trick.

"It was a clone." Jesse added this shocker and awaited Monika's reaction.

"A clone? Is that possible? I thought they were just in science fiction books. We can't clone." Though it seemed ridiculous, inside Monika was beginning to understand that this was the only explanation. She fell silent.

"I know it sounds wild, but the Major told me that the military had been secretly working on it for years and they not only can clone a person, they can transfer their memory as well. He said they had cloned me, but until now I didn't really believe it. It all makes sense."

"Sense? What do you mean?" Monika wanted to hear his rationalization.

"Somehow they have developed a method to perfectly duplicate anyone they want. Imagine what that could mean."

"But people would know."

"Know what? It's so perfect. Every memory. Every bit of personality. Every experience. Every emotion. All uploaded from the original to a clone. Nobody could possible know."

"But what about their soul?"

"What about their soul? No one knows what that is anyway. At least in the living world. Even if the clone had a unique soul, it would be dominated by the uploaded memory of the original.

The upload would be the part that we know of as that person. The rest wouldn't matter. It would be too insignificant and deeply placed. No one would know the difference."

"But why would they do it? Why clone someone?" Monika hadn't made the connection. Her mind was still groggy and she was disoriented from the experience of being kidnapped and imprisoned here.

"Power and money for starters. If they have managed to save and upload a person's identity, what's to stop them from making slight alterations that would make the clone unconsciously controllable by them. They could do anything they want." Jesse finally appreciated what Major Britin had told him. "Of course. That's it."

"What?"

Jesse's last statement didn't make sense to her. She was still trying to accept that she had been with Jesse's clone for an afternoon and never suspected. He seemed like a nice guy. She continued examining her experiences since her arrival in Florida, as Jesse explained.

"They're going to substitute a clone for the President and then control him."

There was silence as the implications of what Jesse said sank in.

"So these are the bad guys," Monika said.

"Yep. It's the perfect coup. No fight. No bloodshed. Nobody knows."

"So this is a plot within the military?" Monika found it hard to accept this was happening in modern day America.

"Probably a small group of fanatics. Each with their own Machiavellian political philosophy that justifies their cause. The Major thinks he's saving the nation. At least that's the impression I got."

"How could they get away with it?"

"They must have some strong connections. The Major isn't the brains behind this plan."

"No. I mean how can they get to the President to clone him and then make the switch?"

"They've already cloned him, from DNA samples from his years in the service. All they need now is to download his memory and then they can complete the duplication."

"How are they going to get to the President? There's Secret Service always protecting him."

Jesse had considered this as well. The President was never far from protection. He was always accompanied by…

"That's why," Jesse spoke his thoughts out loud. "That's why they need me."

Monika watched and listened.

"The President is coming here, to Ft. Jefferson on Friday. I, the clone, am his underwater guide in the moat. I have top security clearance and the moat can be only viewed from both sides. There won't be anyone other than the President and me under the water. He will be alone. It's pretty murky water near the bottom of the moat. There will be plenty of opportunities to make a change without anyone knowing. That's their plan. They're gonna use the clone and trigger him to take the President deep into the moat and at some prearranged spot exchange the President with the clone."

"What about the memory download?"

"I don't know how they plan to do that, but I'm sure they figured it out. It wouldn't take them long. Once they've physically exchanged them, they could do the download anytime."

"Maybe he'll end up here with us," Monika chortled.

"No. I don't think so." Jesse became serious.

"Why not?" Monika already knew the answer.

"They aren't gonna to let us survive to tell."

"And they'll replace us with clones so no one will ever know." Monika understood. It was a perfect plan.

"Exactly."

They both fell silent at the realization of their fate.

"You know. They made more than one clone of you. Maybe there are clones of other people. Maybe the Major and these soldiers are clones. Maybe they're not mad at all, but under the control of one man." Monika mused, though she wondered what type of man would have that power and wealth. She didn't realize how close to the truth she had come.

"How do you know?"

"I don't, but it seems to make sense. I mean, if you can clone anyone you like and make modifications to control them, then why try to convince and manipulate the real person. It's too risky. It's easier to just clone the people you need and get rid of the originals. Then there's no more problems. The clones are programmed without consciously knowing they're programmed or cloned for that matter. If something goes wrong and they're caught, so what. They would never reveal anything, because they wouldn't know anything to reveal. They would all be programmed that way. Whoever's behind this is a really smart cookie. This isn't some minor coup. There's much more at stake here." Monika had had an incredible insight.

"How do you know there's more than one clone of me?" He focused on this part of what Monika said.

"You drowned in Pompano. I found you in the water." The memory of that event still caused her to squirm. It would be haunting her for a long time, but somehow it was less frightening now that she saw the dead body as a clone.

"Drowned?"

"Yeah. I don't know how or why, but you showed up dead in the water."

"Maybe it was an earlier prototype and they

were trying to get rid of it at sea. Unfortunately it washed up on shore. We have to get out of here and stop them before it's too late. But who can we trust?" Jesse was uncertain.

"If we can get out of here, I know who we can trust: my fiancé."

"Your fiancé? We're dealing with some pretty powerful stuff here."

"He's a CIA agent in Los Angeles. He can help. We can trust him. He'll know what to do."

"Then all we have to do is get out of here, and I don't see how we're going to do that."

Monika had a sudden idea. She bent down to her shoe and pulled out the cylindrical piece of metal. She stood back up and held the piece of metal with her thumb and index finger in the window so Jesse could see.

"What's that?"

"It's our key outa here." She smiled. She could pick any lock as long as she had the right tool. She had learnt this skill during her adolescence from an old boyfriend want-a-be Harry Houdini. He used to like to handcuff her and lock her up and see how long it took her to escape. They used to compete with each other. She always managed to escape faster than him in whatever new trick he learnt. That was many years ago now. Monika had always prided herself on being a better escape artist than her boyfriend. Finally, after all those adolescent years of fooling around, these tricks were about to pay off. "When should we try?"

"I was meant to report here on Wednesday."

"That's what Jess," she used the shortened name for the clone, "said. He said he was going out of town for a few days on Wednesday."

"That means they'll all leave here Wednesday and head for Jefferson. It's standard protocol. They're always in place before the President's arrival to double check and secure everything."

"What will they do with us?"

"I think they're just going to leave us, and let us starve to death. They won't leave anyone here to guard us. There won't be a need."

Monika touched her finger to her belly button and found the scab that she had noticed earlier. Now it was beginning to fit. They had taken a DNA sample from her. All they needed now was to get her memory and she could be successfully duplicated. A chill of fear ran through her.

"So we should try tomorrow."

"Yes. They'll probably feed us and then leave. They don't want to alarm us beforehand." Jesse's scenario made sense.

Suddenly there was the sound of a door opening and footsteps coming down the corridor.

Monika and Jesse looked at one another through their windows and without speaking understood each other. Quickly they went from their cell doors and cornered themselves in their cells on their beds. Monika placed the cylindrical piece of metal back into her shoe. They both waited, listening intently like scared animals to the footsteps coming closer. Finally the footsteps stopped in front of their cells.

Monika squatted tensely on the metal bed. The sound of a key twisting in her locked door became loudly audible. It was as if every sound in this dark place was magnified. The door opened outward and two soldiers entered her cell. They were big men in their twenties, each in fatigues and looking remarkably alike in their musculature and buzz cut hair.

"The doctor wants to see you." One of the soldiers roughly called out.

Monika instantly realized that they wanted her memories. She whimpered as the two brutish men approached her. She pushed herself as far away from them as she could. One of the men had gauze in his hand and was holding it out in front of him. The other was closing in to grab hold and subdue her.

"Noooooooo!" she screamed out as the one soldier grabbed her and pulled her towards the other who forced the gauze over her face while he held the back of her head and kept the gauze in place.

"Leave her alone you bastards," Jesse was up and at his cell door shouting through the barred window.

"Shut up asshole. Or it'll be you next," the soldier that was holding onto Monika as she struggled replied to Jesse vulgarly.

"If you hurt her. I'll come after you." Jesse was helpless to do anything, but the threat helped relieve the frustration of his impotence.

Monika tasted the same bittersweet flavor as she had in her struggle with her abductor at the Sandy Reef Resort. Gradually she felt the soporific effect of the drug enter her system. There was nothing she could do to stop it.

The soldiers ignored Jesse and focused on a weakening Monika. Within seconds she was unconscious. The soldier with the gauze withdrew his hand from her face. The other picked Monika up, and they left the cell. They left the cell door open and started back down the corridor.

Jesse watched as Monika, unconscious and thrown over the soldier's shoulder, was being carried off. For the first time he caught a good glimpse of her. She was pretty, and he guessed, in her late twenties. He hoped she would be okay. He knew where the soldiers were taking her. They wanted to download her memory. Monika and Jesse had surmised the situation correctly. Somehow they had to escape and stop them.

After the sound of the soldiers' footsteps faded away, Jesse went back and plumped himself on the bed. The first ray of hope that he had had in a long time was growing within him. He knew that Monika would soon be returned to her cell. Once she recovered they could make their escape plan.

He knew this base well. Once they got out of the brig, they would go up to the main level and then out from the building. The base was right in Key West on the southeast side of the Key. They could disappear into the city amongst the crowd of tourists that were there this time of year. Then Monika could get in touch with her fiancé. The plan should work. There wouldn't be many guards on the abandoned base to stop them. No one would expect them to break out of the brig, assuming that Monika could pick their cell locks. He hoped she could. Their lives depended upon it.

He sat back and thought about his little dive shop in Key Largo. He missed it and the life he had there. When this was all over he was going to go for a long dive and get away from this crazy world.

- - - - - - - - - - - - - - -

The two soldiers arrived at the doctor's lab. They knocked on the door.

"Come in," Doctor Pearl called out. He was making the final adjustments to his equipment in preparation of Monika's arrival. Once her memories were downloaded, he would have all he needed to complete the cloning process. The DNA sample he had taken from her when she had first arrived here unconscious was already being processed.

Monika was carried in.

"Good. Put her there." He indicated the same

chair that Jesse had, but only a short while before, occupied. "And strap her in tight. We don't want anything to happen to our star patient."

The soldiers put her in the chair and started to strap her in. The doctor swabbed her forehead with disinfectant and then punctured her skin with a syringe and began to administer the local anesthetic. The procedure would be over in about half an hour. Monika would be placed unharmed back in her cell before she awakened.

Chapter 8

The fist twelve notes of 'Take Me Out to the Ball Game' began to play on the small cell phone. At first it was not very loud but, with each repetition of the seven notes, its volume grew.

"Hello," a man answered.

James had not heard from Monika on Monday night as he had expected. He decided to call her today. It was just after lunch, Florida time. He had arrived late this morning and was just starting his day in Los Angeles.

"Hello?" James was startled that a man was answering Monika's phone. He remained calm and tried not to show his surprise. "Is Monika there?"

"Who is this?" the man gruffly asked.

James did not like the tone of the question and, hardening his reply, "James Anstey. Her fiancé."

"Oh Mr. Anstey. I'm Detective Swan..." He became nicer.

"Yes."

"...Ah..." there was hesitation at Swan's end as he stumbled for the rights words.

"What's wrong? Where's Monika?" James recognized the hesitation.

"That's just it. I don't know."

"What do you mean?" James' heart skipped a beat.

"She seems to have disappeared without a trace."

"Disappeared?" James was stunned.

"Yes."

"Where? When?"

"I'm not exactly sure, but it looks like it was last night. She checked into the Sandy Reef Resort here in Key Largo and hasn't been seen since."

"Maybe she's gone on to visit friends." James wasn't aware of her knowing any one in Key Largo, but he knew that she had gone to Florida before him to explore and see the sights. He knew she was going to the Coral Reef Park and maybe she met some old friends.

"I don't think so. She left her purse, wallet, phone and all her clothes. She ordered dinner from Room Service, but never touched it. There's no sign of a struggle. The Resort called us in to investigate, but we don't have any leads."

It was very strange. Monika would not go off without her purse. He searched his feelings for any connection to her. He felt she was alive, but that was as much as he sensed.

"Did anyone see anything?" James put aside his personal feelings and his tone became professional.

"We're still trying to find out. All we know is, she spent some time diving yesterday. She used a local Dive Master."

"What did he say?"

"I was just about to go and talk to him." Detective Swan noted the tone James used to ask the question. "Mr. Anstey what do you do?"

"I'm with the CIA in Los Angeles." Under the circumstances James decided to be up front with Swan.

"Oh." Swan thought he sensed some police connection and was pleased that he picked it up.

"Well if you like I can call you after I speak with the guy." He extended professional courtesy.

"I'd appreciate that."

"I'd be happy to."

"By the way, Detective Swan. If there is anything my office can do to help, let me know." James didn't want to insult the local authorities, but he was in a position to give incredible support if it was requested. He would do anything for

Monika.

"No. I've got it under control. There's nothing to go on yet. Maybe later. Thanks." Swan wasn't offended. If the situation was reversed he would offer the same assistance. "Don't worry. She'll be okay. I'll find her." Swan's instincts told him that Monika was gone, but alive.

"Thanks." James appreciated the assurance.

"Give me your number. I'll get back to you in a couple of hours."

James gave Swan his office number. He wrote it down on a slip of paper and put it into his pants pocket. They said good-bye and hung up.

Swan did not wear the dress of the usual police detective. He was much more casual, wearing a full cabana style short sleeve shirt that had a floral pattern of yellows, greens and blues, and khaki shorts. He had on a pair of tan 'Jesus' sandals. His legs were hairy but well proportioned; his upper body lean, tanned and in shape. He wore a silver box-link chain around his neck. The first two buttons of his shirt were undone. A Saint Christopher medallion hung upon the chain. He had on a pair of fifties style Ray Bans and longish dark hair. Swan, in his mid forties, seemed older than his age. He had come out of the Navy and had been working here in the Keys for ten years and was a veteran of the force. In Key Largo he could get away with his unkempt appearance. The Keys, though a part of the United States, was another world.

Later that afternoon, Swan's sun-faded car pulled up in front of Jess's Dive Tours. Margaret had given Jess's message to the detective and told him about the missed dive. Jess came out of the shop as Swan got out of the car.

"Hi. Jess."

"Hi Dan. What brings you out here?" Jess knew Dan well. They had both served in the navy.

"Business. I want to know about the girl that missed her dive."

"What's up?" Jess was bringing a bag of equipment out to his pick-up. He threw the bag into the back and turned to face Dan.

"She's disappeared."

"Oh yeah. She stiffed me. I thought I was a better judge of people."

"What do you mean?" The two stood facing each other in casual conversation.

"I took her out to White Bank for a couple of hours. She seemed to have a great time and wanted to go again today. So I told her we'd settle up later."

"Was there anything wrong? Any sign of upset or problem?"

"No. Nothing. She was having a great time. Couldn't wait to get out to the dive. What do you think has happened to her?"

"I don't know. She left everything at the resort."

"Maybe she just took off."

"No. She left all her money, ID and clothes. She wouldn't get very far without them."

"Oh, what's happened to her?"

"I don't know, but it's beginning to look like an abduction."

"Abduction? Here in the Keys? Why? Who is she?"

"I don't know. She's just an average person. There's nothing unusual about her that I can see. It's really strange."

"I'll say."

"Where are you going?" Swan asked, finally noticing Jess's bag in the truck.

"Key West. I'm doing duty over the next couple of days."

"The President's visit?" Dan knew all about the upcoming Presidential visit. He and his department had been briefed weeks ago.

"Yeah. I'm taking him on a dive at Jefferson." Jess was not concerned about telling. Dan was a police detective and already knew about the trip in general, and he was a close Navy friend. They shared many secrets.

"Mingling with the White House crowd now are you? You'll have to put up your rates," Dan joked.

"Yeah. That would be a nice bonus." Jess smiled, but seemed distracted.

"You seem nervous. How come?" Dan noted the mood.

"I don't know. It's probably just stage fright. All the press and commotion that will be there. You know me. I like my quiet life here."

"Yeah. It is nice, but I wouldn't say no to your assignment. It's a great recommendation. It'll be good for business."

"Yeah. You're right. It's just nerves."

It was not like Jess to have nerves. Dan had never known him to react this way. But people change. Even he was not the same person he used to be. He was calmer and not as reckless as during his Navy days.

"Well good luck. When are you coming back?"

"Sunday. I'm going to spend a day in Key West after the visit."

"Sounds good. Give me a call when you get back. We'll go for a drink." Dan put out his hand.

"Okay. I will." Jess took his friend's hand. They shook.

"Take care of the President now. The future of our country's in your hands." Dan walked to his car, got in and started the engine. He waved as he pulled out, heading back to the Sandy Reef Resort. He wanted to have one last look at Monika's room.

- - - - - - - - - - - - - - -

It was a comfortable room. Detective Swan was sitting on the couch looking out over the ocean. He was trying to make sense of Monika's disappearance. There had to be a clue that he had missed. He went over everything in his head. The conversation with Jess, Margaret, and the Resort staff. Nothing. He believed that Monika had been abducted, but he couldn't understand why or by whom.

Frustrated by the case, he picked up the phone and dialed James' number. It was six fifteen Florida time. James would still be at work.

"Agent Anstey," James answered after one ring. He was waiting for the call from Swan.

"Mr. Anstey. Dan Swan in Key Largo."

"Hi Dan. What have you got?"

"Nothing. I spoke to the dive shop, but everything checks out. Your fiancée was planning a dive today but never showed up."

"I don't understand. There has to be someone who saw something, some clue?"

"I'm sorry, but there's nothing. It's clean."

"So what's your hunch?"

"I think she's been abducted. I think she opened the door to whoever it was and was surprised. That's why there's no forced entry. I think it was well planned. They probably drugged her and that's why there's no sign of struggle."

"But who? Why?"

"That's the million dollar question. I hope you don't mind my asking, but was everything all right between you two?"

"Yes, fine. There are no problems."

"Why did she come here without you?"

"I couldn't get any extra time and she wanted a few days alone before we met up in Key West. We're going to spend a week with my parents."

"I see." Dan didn't know what to say.

"I'm coming there, as soon as I can."

"There's really nothing you can do. It's probably better to stay put and wait a day or so. Maybe there'll be a ransom demand." He didn't want James to make an unnecessary trip, but knew he would not be able to stop him.

"There would have been something by now if this was a kidnapping. You and I both know that." James was correct. There should have been some call or message if this was a kidnapping.

"Yeah. That's what bothers me." Dan did not have to explain why. James understood.

"I'm taking the next flight. I'll call you when I arrive."

"Let me know your flight number and I'll meet you."

"Thanks. I'll get back to you." James hung up.

Swan sighed as he hung up the phone. He sank back into the couch. He wondered what this was all about. His gut was gnawing away at him. There was something very odd about this case.

- - - - - - - - - - - - - - - -

Not long after Monika had been chloroformed and taken away by the two soldiers, the sound of footsteps could be heard along the corridor to the brig. The same two soldiers were bringing her back to her cell. She was unconscious. The doctor had injected her with a strong sedative. She would not awake until the morning.

Jesse, upon hearing the sounds, hurried to his barred window and strained to see down the corridor. Gradually he saw the two men. They were carrying an unconscious Monika. He did not say a thing, but watched as they carried her by and into the cell. They placed her on the bed and came out of the cell. One soldier started walking down the corridor while the other closed and locked the door.

"Don't worry. Your girlfriend's just having a nap. She'll be fine tomorrow." He laughed and without even looking at Jesse started after his partner down the corridor.

Once they were gone, Jesse called out, "Monika? Are you all right? Monika?"

He waited but got no response. He moved away from the cell door and sat back on his bed. There was nothing he could do until she awoke. Tomorrow they would have to make their attempt to escape. Time was running out.

- - - - - - - - - - - - - - -

James was now approaching the east shores of Key Largo. His boss had been in a meeting and could not be disturbed. James had not waited to get permission to leave. He had left the office and hurriedly made all the required arrangements. He had taken a flight to Miami, which left at 5:20 PM

California time. He had phoned Detective Swan from the plane to give him the details. Swan had given him the name of an old friend with a small seaplane company that could fly him out of Miami to Key Largo tonight. Everything had been arranged. The seaplane would drop him at the Sandy Reef Resort and they would meet later.

James was tired as the seaplane jerked about in its approach in the dark to land on the bay in front of the Sandy Reef Resort. It was a run down small four man capacity craft. Its exterior paint was soiled and there was gray duct tape wrapped around one of the pontoons. It amazed him that they had made it from Miami. The pilot was a man who looked like he should have retired twenty years ago. He was unshaven, gray haired and wore an old tattered leather flight jacket and an old worn St. Louis ball cap which had an older out of date team logo sewn into its front.

The pilot was a chatty geriatric man, and did not seem to care if James conversed or not. James had not paid much attention to the constant barrage of conversation that spewed from him since leaving Miami.

The water in front of the Sandy Reef was calm and illuminated by the full moon. The bright lights of the resort glittered on the ocean. The dock was lit up in anticipation of the seaplane's arrival.

"Hang on," was the only warning given before

their contact with the water. The pilot stopped his chatter and devoted his attention to the water below. James did not like to have to make a landing like this in such dark conditions, but the pilot seemed pleasantly amused by the challenge and his passenger's trepidation.

The plane bounced twice upon the ocean before coming into solid contact with the water. The engine roared as the pilot tried to slow the craft. The roll of the water caused the plane to toss back and forth. The plane somehow managed to taxi to the dock.

Detective Swan was standing on the dock as the plane arrived. There was a creaking sound when the side hatch opened. James jumped out, brief-case in hand from the plane to the dock. The noise from the running engine forced Swan to shout.

"Hi. James?" He took James' hand and steadied him.

"Dan?"

"Welcome to Paradise." Dan smiled, stretched over, slammed the hatch shut then banged loudly on the side of the plane.

The seaplane's engine revved up and the plane began to pull away from the dock. The wind from the propeller blew the two men's clothes, making them flap uncontrollably. The men remained still and watched as the plane pointed out to sea and began its take-off run.

The plane roared louder and louder as it picked

up power and speed. The splash from the water created a trail as it skimmed along the surface. Within moments it was airborne and disappeared into the cloudless night sky . The Sandy Reef was peaceful once more.

"How was your flight?" Dan asked as they walked along the dock to the resort office.

"Fine to Miami, but *that* was an experience."

"Oh old Raymond. He's a little eccentric at times. An old war veteran from World War II. The only other way to get here is to drive the two hours from Miami, but I thought you wouldn't mind getting here sooner. Hope it wasn't that bad." Dan grinned. He could imagine what the flight with Raymond was like, but Raymond was one of the best, even in his seventies.

"No. No. It was fine, just a little different."

"I've arranged everything. You have a room here. Let's check-in and then get over to your fiancée's cabin." Dan changed the subject. "Have you eaten?"

"I had something on the plane to Miami."

"Good."

The two of them walked across the lawn and entered the main lobby. James noted how, even in the dark, the resort had a charm to it. Under other circumstances he would have loved it here.

- - - - - - - - - - - - - - -

After checking-in, James and Dan hurried off to check on Monika's cabin.

"Nothing's been moved. It was all like this when we found it. I thought you'd like to see it that way."

"Thanks." James scrutinized the room for any type of clue that could solve this mystery. "It looks like a very professional job, doesn't it?"

"That's what I thought. Whoever took her was good. But I still don't know why they wanted her. It doesn't make sense."

"No. It doesn't," James pondered as he visually searched every aspect of the room. "I don't get it."

They both fell silent. There was really nothing here that could lead them further. It was baffling. They both silently wondered if some crazed pervert had taken her, if she would show up abused and dead in some ditch along the roadway. James didn't want to think about that possibility. He shook himself. He searched his deepest inner feelings. She did not feel dead. He still felt her alive within him. He still felt a connection to her. She was nearby and unharmed. He couldn't explain the feeling. He just knew it. It wasn't wishful thinking. It was a psychic sensing of her and her well being.

Dan, realizing James' dismay broke their silence. "I could use a drink. What about you?"

"Yeah." James was physically and emotionally exhausted. He missed Monika and wanted to be with her, but he realized if he didn't keep control, he would be of no help, whatever that help might be, to detective Swan or Monika. He pulled himself together. There was a job to be done and he was a cop with the best resources in the world to back him up. He would solve this mystery and find her alive.

"That sounds like a good idea. Know any good places?"

"Follow me."

Chapter 9

"**G**ood morning Mr. Ehrlich. You're right on time." Major Britin and his men were preparing to leave for Ft. Jefferson. They were all in fatigues, including Jess.

Jess had left around nine and made the trip down to Key West in good time. He had been allowed onto the base by a sole guard and had driven up the long driveway to the south side of the building. The base was unkempt. The building, made from cinder blocks with a veneer plastered over, was sun beaten. In places the light gray plaster had deteriorated, exposing the cement brick below. The tropical vegetation that grew around and along the building was not being tended as it

had once been in the Base's heyday. It was growing wild. There was a large lawn in the front of
the structure that was yellow from lack of water
and attention. Palm trees lined the driveway to the
building. There was debris from them littering the
roadway.

Jess drove past the building farther south. The
south side of the base faced the ocean. To his left
was a parking lot that abutted the building. To his
right was an old dock and the vast ocean. Three
small navy craft were moored along the dock.
Jess parked his pick-up near the building, got out
and walked across the short distance to the
docked boats. About a dozen men were loading
up the last few bags of their equipment onto the
boats. Jess had arrived just in time. The Major,
supervising the operation, had been standing
about fifteen feet away from the boats.

"Good morning, Sir. Captain Ehrlich reporting
for duty, Sir." Jess came up to and saluted him.

"Where's your gear Captain?"

"In the truck Sir." Jess did not know the Major
well and there was a formality to their meeting.

"Get it stowed on the first boat. That's yours."
Britin pointed out the boat.

"Yes Sir."

"Are you ready?"

"Yes Sir."

"We will be at Jefferson in a few hours. I've put
all the other equipment that you'll need for the

President on board. You'll have the day tomorrow to set-up. Any questions?"

"Sir. Are we still scheduled for return on Saturday?"

"Yes."

"Thank you Sir." Jess saluted and went back to get his gear from the pick-up.

"As soon as your gear is loaded, we'll cast off," he shouted as Jess left. Everything was going as planned. He took his sat-phone out of his pocket and punched a speed dial button. He placed the phone to his right ear and waited as the call connected and a phone at the other end rang.

"Brookland," came a voice.

"Colonel Brookland, Sir. We're all set. We will be at Jefferson this afternoon."

"Good Major. And the Dive Master?"

"No problems Sir. He doesn't know a thing."

"Good. Let's hope the doctor's changes click-in at the right time."

"Sir. They will."

"The President is set to arrive by chopper on schedule. Will your men be in place?"

"No problem Sir. We'll have it disabled."

"Good. I'll see you Saturday at the base according to plan." Brookland disconnected.

Britin put his phone back into his pocket. The operation was running smoothly. He didn't anticipate any difficulties.

- - - - - - - - - - - - - - -

"Monika. Monika," Jesse called louder.

Monika was slowly awakening when she heard his call.

"Ugh," she moaned and opened her eyes. Her head was woozy. She put her right hand to her forehead. She hoped she was having a bad dream, but the stench of the brig rapidly sobered her back to reality.

"Monika. Are you awake?"

She gradually got up from the bed and stumbled over to the cell door. Her clothes were wrinkled. She felt dirty.

"Yeah. I'm okay." She leaned against the door, brushed back her hair and responded. "What day is it?"

"Wednesday. It must be around lunchtime. You've been out for hours."

"What happened to me?"

"They hooked you up to a machine and… That's how they downloaded me. You'll be okay. You've been drugged."

"Yeah…" Monika was cut-off from saying more by the sound of footsteps coming from the other end of the corridor.

It was lunchtime. Without saying a word both Jesse and Monika moved away from their doors and returned to their beds. As usual the steps grew louder as they approached their cells and then abruptly stopped. Keys rustled and each of their doors was opened in turn. Monika's was first. She pretended to be asleep. A young soldier put a tray of food on the floor of the cell and left without uttering a word. He closed and re-locked her door.

When the soldier entered Jesse's cell he also put the tray on the floor, but noticing Jesse awake and sitting on the bed, broke his normal silence.

"Lunch." He stood back up after placing the tray on the floor and regarded Jesse.

"What's going on Corporal?" Jesse identified his rank.

"I'm ordered not to speak to you." He was very young and appeared to be a new recruit.

"Isn't that a little odd?"

"I have my orders."

"Tell the Major I want to talk to him."

"They've all gone. You'll have to wait 'til Saturday."

Jesse did not respond. He remained in thought. He watched as the soldier turned and left. The cell door was closed and locked. His steps could be heard as he went back down the corridor. In about an hour he would return to pick up the trays. Jesse waited several minutes and then resumed his position at his cell door.

"Monika. He's gone."

Monika, now more awake, got up and went back to her door being careful to step around the tray of food and drink. She was hungry, but not for beans and water. She looked through the window over to Jesse.

"Now's the time."

"What about him?"

"If you can get these doors opened, I've got a plan. We need to get his keys."

"What?"

"Don't worry about that now. Have you got that piece of metal?"

Monika bent down and felt in her left shoe. Her fingertips ran across the cylindrical object. She was pleased that it had not fallen out when she had been taken to the lab. She pulled it out and rose back up to the window. "Yes. It's here." She held it at the window to show him.

"Do you think you can do it?"

"No problem. I've picked harder locks than these." She wasn't really sure, but she didn't let him hear her doubt.

"Okay. I'll keep a look-out."

Monika turned her back and leaned on the door. She knew what to do. She needed to bend the metal cylinder into an 'L' shape, but the metal was too rigid to bend by hand. She did not possess that kind of strength. She considered what she could use. She needed something like a vise. She looked around the dimly lit cell, but couldn't find anything suitable. Then she had an idea. She turned back to face the door and examined its trim. Along the hinge side of the rusty gray metal door there was a crack between the door and its jam. She took the cylindrical piece of metal and forced it into the crack. She managed to insert it about three quarters of an inch. It was firmly held in place. Now she needed something to strike and bend it, like a hammer. She looked down to the metal tray on the floor that held her food. That would do the job. She bent down and pulled the tray, spilling the water and plate of beans onto the floor. There were no utensils. Prisoners were expected to eat with their hands. The food and drink made a mess on the floor, but she didn't care. Picking up the tray she grabbed it along its edge and returned to the metal cylinder. She began to hammer at the part of the metal that protruded from the crack.

On her first couple of hits nothing happened. But the loud noise that echoed throughout the brig worried her. She stopped and listened for footsteps.

"It's okay. He can't hear. Hurry," Jesse, who was watching the corridor through his window, called out to her.

Monika began again. This time she used more strength. She realized that it was all or nothing; that she had to hit the object harder regardless of the noise it would make. The tray struck and made a loud noise as she directed it to the cylinder. This time the cylinder began to bend.

"Keep going," Jesse encouraged.

She hit it several more times until it was bent flush with the door. She tried to remove the piece of metal from the door, but could not budge it. It was jammed in place. She threw the tray down and picked up the empty metal cup that had rolled next to her bed. Using the lip of the cup she managed to pry the cylinder out of the crack of the door. Gradually she pried it out and examined her workmanship. It was perfect. She had made a tool to pick the lock.

Taking the tool in her right hand, she got down on her knees and checked the keyhole. These older style locks were very simple in their construction. They were very much like the locking mechanism on handcuffs. All she had to do was find the lever within and twist it with the tool.

Carefully she inserted the long end into the keyhole. It easily fit. Her eyes went into a blank stare as she tried to visualize the mechanism inside the door in her mind. Carefully she prodded, pushed, turned and then twisted the tool. After several minutes of fiddling, she found the correct spot within the lock and, using the short end of the tool for leverage, twisted and jerked the tool upward. She was careful not to work the tool too hard in fear that it might break, but the metal was strong and took the force. There followed a click and a clank of the lock as the lever within opened.

She removed the tool and took in a breath, hoping she had accomplished her task. She leaned up against the door and gingerly pushed. There was a creak as the cell door opened. Monika grinned a smile of self praise and satisfaction. The door opened wide and she stared over to Jesse.

"Congratulations. Now get mine open."

Monika stepped out and looked down the corridor. There was no one in sight. She crossed over to Jesse's cell and inserted her tool into his lock. She was much more confident this time and it was not long before the mechanism was unlocked. She pulled the door open and stepped back. Before her was Jesse—the same one from Pompano and Key Largo. He was wearing faded blue jeans and a blue T-shirt. He had obviously been there for a while. His blonde hair was dirty. Everything about him, other than a growth of beard that she had not seen from her cell window, was the same as the other Jess's. She felt like she knew him well, but they had never really met.

"Hi. I don't think we've met," she joked.

Jesse stepped out and embraced her. She noticed his rank odor, but didn't outwardly let him know.

"Not bad. Not bad at all." He was impressed by Monika's abilities. He wondered what else she was capable of.

"What do we do now?" She wondered if she smelt as bad as he.

"We're going to play a game of hide-n-seek."

- - - - - - - - - - - - - - -

The ocean had a gentle swell. The three naval boats were half way to their destination. They powered along at full speed and were in a 'V' formation like a flock of Canada geese flying south for the winter. Long white lines of their wake trailed off behind them. The water reflected the hot bright sun and the blue of the sky. Not another craft could be seen in the vicinity. This was not a popular tourist area. It was too remote and the waters were said to be infested with modern day pirates and drug runners. It was a perfect location for their operation.

- - - - - - - - - - - - - - -

Footsteps could be heard echoing down the corridor of the brig as the same soldier returned to pick up the prisoner's trays. He came up to Monika's cell first and opened the door. He saw the mess of food all over the floor and shrugged.

"If you want to starve that's fine by me, but I ain't cleaning up that slop," he spoke out in disgust, fully expecting to see Monika sitting on her bed. But she wasn't. She wasn't in the cell—but that was impossible. She had to be here! The soldier rushed into the cell. He didn't understand what had happened to her. He visually searched the tiny space. There was nowhere to hide. He would be in trouble if she had gotten away, but he didn't know how she could have done it.

Panicking, he turned and ran across to Jesse's cell and looked through the small barred window. He could not see Jesse either. He fumbled with his keys as he tried to open Jesse's cell door. In his hurry he did not notice that the lock was open. He pulled upon the door and let his keys recoil back up onto his belt along the chain that attached them.

Jesse and Monika were tightly pressed, on opposite sides, against the wall adjacent to the cell door. They remained silent and held their breath as the soldier was unlocking the door. They did not want to give themselves away. Their hearts raced. Droplets of perspiration formed on their foreheads.

The door opened and the soldier stepped in. There was no prisoner to be seen. He walked into the center of the tiny room and stopped. Somehow they had both escaped.

As soon as the guard entered the cell, Jesse jumped out from the wall and pounced on him from behind. The soldier was completely caught off-guard. They both fell to the floor. Jesse had his left arm in a strangle hold about the soldier's neck. The soldier was struggling and trying to break out of the death grip that held him. Jesse strained as he tightened his suffocating hold. Monika backed away from the two squirming men to the relative safety of a corner. It was a horrifying sight. Her senses heightened, she listened for anyone else coming down the corridor who might assist the soldier, but no one came.

The soldier kicked and fought. Jesse had him. He was unable to break free. Jesse used all his power to restrain the man and tighten his hold on him. He put every ounce of his strength into the effort. For a moment Monika wondered if the soldier would break free. The two squirmed around the floor, but Jesse did not let go. It was a frightening sight for Monika to see. She brought her hand to her mouth and opened her eyes wide.

After one final furious struggle the soldier stopped fighting. His hands gripped onto Jesse's arm but he was unable to loosen Jesse's strangle hold from cutting his breathing off. Jesse continued his clamp-like grip and began to shake and twist the soldier's head and neck. The soldier suddenly went limp and let go of Jesse's arm. Jesse waited a couple of seconds before letting go his hold. He wasn't taking any chances. He wanted to be sure that the soldier was not playing possum. After several more moments Jesse fell back on the floor panting, trying to recover from the fight.

"Is he dead?" Monika blurted from the corner. She had never seen such a nightmarish display of brutality.

"No…" Jesse was still out of breath. "Just unconscious. He'll be okay…Just a little sore when he wakes up. He'll…need a good chiropractor though." Jesse smiled at her, trying to lighten the mood. He realized from the strained look upon her face that she was shocked by his display of human barbarism.

"Oh." She wasn't sure how to react.

"Get the keys. We have to hurry." Jesse was

almost recovered.

Monika squeamishly stepped over Jesse and knelt by the soldier. She quickly found and undid the keys from the soldier's belt and stood back up.

"Let me help you." She offered a helping hand to Jesse.

"Thanks." He took her hand and got up. His shirt was stained with sweat.

"Now what?"

"We've got to get out of here. Let's go."

"What about him?"

"We'll lock him in. He'll be okay."

Jesse went into the corridor first. Monika followed and closed the door. Using the soldier's keys, she locked him in. They both stood a moment in the corridor and listened. The brig was quiet. No one else had heard the commotion. Jesse broke their silence.

"We'll make our way up to the next level and then out."

"How many men will there be?"

"Not many. They've all left for Jefferson. There might only be one or two left to secure the base. We should be okay."

"Let's go." Monika was as ready as she was going to be.

Jesse took Monika's hand and led the way. They moved stealthily down the corridor, listening to every sound that they heard, feeling exposed and vulnerable.

At the end of the corridor was the metal door. Jesse tried the handle but the door was locked. Monika came forward with the keys and started the trial and error process of finding the correct key. There were about a dozen keys on the chain. After trying a couple of them, she found the right one and managed to unlock the door. She pulled it open. It revealed the stairwell they had both been brought down. She stopped and they both listened. There wasn't a sound. They entered into the dark zigzag stairwell and proceeded up the stairs.

After twenty steps they came to a landing. A dim caged light glowed from the wall. They stopped on the landing and listened, but heard nothing. They continued up the next twenty steps and came to the main floor door. A big 'M' was painted on the door in white. Their hearts were pounding. Slowly Jesse turned the handle and cracked the door open. He peeked through the crack, which revealed the long narrow navy-gray hall of the main floor. There were several closed doors along the hallway that, he assumed, were the old base offices. The offices appeared vacant and no longer in use. There was an empty feel to the place. He waited a few more moments to be sure that there was no one around. Satisfied, he opened the door about half way and ushered Monika into the hallway. He followed after her. They closed the door quietly behind them and stood in the hallway.

At one end of the hallway there was nothing but a dead end. At the other end there was a set of doors. These double doors were chained shut and stood under a red EXIT sign. It was the emergency exit that opened onto the southeast parking lot, though they were not aware of its location.

"There. We'll go out there." Jesse pointed and started toward the doors.

Monika nodded. Jesse started down the hallway. She followed him to the emergency exit. They both stopped in front of the doors.

"See if you can open it." Jesse meant the padlock that held the chain around the door handles.

Monika nervously rifled through the keys again until one finally undid the padlock. She pulled the padlock away and unraveled the chain from the door handles. Jesse had been keeping watch down the hallway.

"What about the alarm?" Monika suddenly realized that the emergency doors might trigger an alarm once opened.

"Maybe. But this place hasn't been used in years. Maybe the alarm's been disconnected. We'll just have to try. If it does go off we'll make a break for it. Just stay close to me." Jesse hadn't considered this outcome, but there was no other option. They had to get away while they could.

Monika grabbed onto one of the door's handles and prayed. She hoped there wasn't an alarm.

"Here goes."

She gingerly pushed upon the handle and heard its clasp open. She hesitated to be sure that no one had heard the noise, but heard no other sound. They had not been discovered. She slowly pushed the door outward and closed her eyes in anticipation of breaking some threshold and tripping the alarm. As she pushed the door open she held her breath. The door opened. There was no alarm. She opened her eyes. A sudden beam of bright sunshine burst in on them.

It was a brilliant day outside. Both Jesse and Monika squinted at this sudden brightness. They had both been in the dark of the brig for a long time and it took a few minutes to fully adjust. Through their squinting, they surveyed the area the door opened onto.

Outside was an old paved parking lot. There were date palm trees along one side of the lot and a roadway to the right. Straight ahead, about a hundred feet away, was a docking area and the ocean. In the lot was one sole parked vehicle.

"That looks like my pick-up." Jesse was surprised to see his vehicle parked next to the building.

"That's the same one I saw at your...I mean the clone's...I mean..."

"I understand. We can use it to get away."

"What about the keys?"

"The doors don't lock and the ignition is worn.

It doesn't need a key to start. I knew there was a reason I kept that old girl." Jesse smiled. He was pleased that his old pick-up could help them.

"So…he…must be here?"

"No. They've all left. He's probably with them at Jefferson by now. Let's make a run for the pick-up. Ready?"

Their eyes better adjusted, they checked from side to side. No one was in sight. The base was truly abandoned.

"Okay." Monika was ready.

They made a dash from the building across the lot to the pick-up. Monika got in the passenger side and Jesse the driver's side. He turned the ignition and the engine began to run.

"See. I told you." Jesse was like a kid. "Let's get out of here."

He put the pick-up in reverse and backed up. Once there was enough room he threw the shifter into drive and they pulled away. He drove along the roadway around the building. The whole area was vacant. They were lucky. Their timing had been right. Major Britin, not believing anyone could escape from the brig, had left only two of his new recruits behind: one at the gate of the base to prevent anyone from trespassing, and the other inside the building to take care of the prisoners— that one Jesse had taken care of. After the operation was successfully completed, Britin had intended to return and deal with the two captives.

As the pick-up followed the road and came around the building, the gate at the main entrance came into view. Though far away, it looked like there was a soldier in the booth.

"There's someone there," Monika drew it to Jesse's attention.

"That's okay. We'll make it." Jesse pushed the accelerator pedal and grabbed firmly onto the wheel. "Hang on." Jesse was determined to get past the guard.

Monika tensed in her seat.

Inside the booth the other soldier left by the Major was sitting reading a paper. Out of the corner of his eye he saw the movement of the pick-up on the base roadway. He looked up. It was the same vehicle that he had let in a few hours ago. He wondered why it was leaving. The Major had given orders that no one was to enter or leave the base until his return. The pick-up was going fast and would soon be at the gate. He stood up from his chair and stepped out of the booth. He moved into the center of the road. He was dressed in fatigues and a sidearm was holstered on his left side. He waved his arms to get their attention and slow the pick-up.

"He's making us stop."

"That's what he thinks. If he starts shooting, duck." Jesse was not going to stop under any circumstances.

The soldier kept waving but the pick-up did not

alter its speed. He became worried that the truck was not going to slow down at all. He identified that there were two people in the vehicle—a man and a woman. He did not recognize either of them. He waved at them to slow down and put his right hand on the butt of his holstered weapon. It made him feel more invincible.

"He's getting his gun," Monika announced.

"Don't worry we'll be okay. Here we go." Jesse floored the accelerator. The pick-up was now traveling fast and they were almost upon the soldier at the barricaded gate.

The soldier could clearly see the two occupants of the pick-up. They were almost at his position. He nervously drew out his weapon and aimed it at the pick-up. He was reluctant to shoot the people, but he would try and disable the pick-up if it didn't slow down and stop. The pick-up was coming straight at him.

"You're going to hit him."

"No. He'll move." They were about fifty feet away and closing.

The soldier could not wait any longer. He fired a round at the pick-up, but it still didn't slow down.

"Get down!" Jesse yelled when he saw the solder discharge his weapon. Monika instantly threw herself down onto the floorboards and cowered. Seconds later a bullet shattered the right-hand mirror.

Jesse swerved to his left and caught a glimpse of the broken side mirror.

"You son-of-a-bitch." He was angry that the soldier had damaged his truck. He kept his foot flat on the ground and aimed directly at the soldier in the road. Nothing was going to stop him now.

The solder was pleased that he had hit the pick-up, but surprised that it had not slowed down. He aimed again and let another round go. This time he did not have as much time to aim. The pick-up was almost upon him. As the shot was fired he jumped out of the pick-up's path.

Jesse winced as he saw the next shot being fired and felt the impact somewhere in the front grill area. The soldier had missed him. The gate ahead was closed. Jesse braced himself for the crash through it.

"Here we go," he forewarned Monika. "We're almost through."

As the soldier jumped from the drive, the pick-up sped by and, with a loud impact, broke through the barrier and the gate to freedom. Jesse knew that the soldier would fire after they passed and that he had to get off the main road. Up ahead was a side street. He immediately turned left onto it.

The soldier scurried to his feet and aimed his gun at the pick-up. He fired indiscriminately until it turned and went out of sight. Gun in hand he stood in the middle of the road stunned at what had just occurred. He considered what he should do. There was no one in authority at the base to contact. He would have to wait until the Major returned. He hoped that he would not be too strongly reprimanded for allowing the pick-up and its occupants out of the base.

"Whew!" Jesse was overjoyed. "We made it. You can come up now. Are you okay?" Jesse began to slow down to a normal speed.

"Yeah. I'm fine." Monika got back into her seat and brushed herself off.

"We'd better go straight to the authorities." He took a right at the next street. Monika noticed its name was Truman Avenue.

"I don't think so." She was following her intuition.

"But we've got to stop them."

"Yeah, but how do we know that they haven't reported us to them, or that they aren't infiltrated with clones?"

"Oh. Yeah. That's possible." Jesse knew she had a point. "So what do we do?"

"Give me a minute."

They drove up Truman. It was a pretty street saturated with lush tropical plants and flowers. The most abundant plant life was the fan palm— it grew everywhere. There were old tall trees and small young stubs.

The houses along the road were more cottage-like and painted in cream colors, predominately off-whites. Monika found it interesting that a lot of the roofs were also white. She was used to the darker red adobe tiles or asphalt shingle roofs of California. The cottages were mostly one story though several were two storied with large verandas. All the houses so far were made of wood. There was a sun-bleached appearance to everything other than the vegetation. There was also a slight New Orleans feel to the place.

As Jesse drove, Monika considered their options. They had to stop the Major and his men, but she wondered how far the conspiracy went. James would know what to do. She needed a phone. She had an idea.

"I know. We can go to James' parents."

"Where do they live?"

"They have a vacation home here."

"They'll be surprised to see us."

"No, they aren't here yet. They actually live in New York and are coming here to spend a week with us. They won't be here 'til Friday and James and I are meant to arrive Saturday."

Jesse didn't respond.

"Do you know…" Monika tried to remember the address that she had written in her address book before leaving Santa Barbara, "Whitehead. Yes. Their place is on Whitehead…118 Whitehead. It's a small renovated cigar maker's cottage." She recalled how unusual she had thought the origins of James' parent's place were when he had first told her about it several weeks ago. She had been intrigued and eager to see it. Now it would offer a safe port in the storm.

"Yeah. We're coming up to it now." Jesse signaled and turned left onto Whitehead.

Whitehead was a very unique street. There were magnificent red flowering trees lining both sides of the street, in front of small, naturally faded and unpainted, clapboard houses. The houses were in all stages of disrepair. Most were single story, but a few were two stories. With their tin roofs, some rusty and others newly renovated, they created a picturesqueness and quaintness that took you away from the real world. It was beautiful. As they drove, Monika marveled at the sight. From behind one of the cottages she saw an old lighthouse come into view.

"What are these trees?"

"Flame Trees."

"They're beautiful."

"Yeah. This is the best time of year to see them."

"And what's that." She pointed to the lighthouse to the right that rose above the house and trees.

The lighthouse was a tan-colored brick tower. She could only see its top third. There was a circular black-railed walkway near its top, and above it a smaller domed roof area. A small ball-like object topped off the roof. It was an odd design.

"That's the old Key West Lighthouse. It's a

museum now."

"It's very pretty here."

"Yeah. Welcome to paradise," Jesse repeated the Conch Republic's slogan. They continued on admiring the sights. Jesse was paying more attention to the house numbers.

"98. 100. There." He drew the next house to her attention. 118. Should we pull in?"

On their right was a beautifully renovated single story cottage. The flame trees seemed fuller here. There was a well-cared-for plush tropical garden in front, and tall palm trees looming over the home. It was very romantic.

"Yes. It'll be okay."

Jesse pulled into the driveway and turned off the engine. The driveway was hidden from outside view by the large trees and plants of the property. It was a very private place. No wonder James loved it here. It felt like a secluded island paradise. They both got out of the pick-up and stood on the black driveway. Monika noted her disheveled appearance and felt out of place in such a lovely well-groomed place.

"Let's go around back and see if we can get in." She knew that no one was there, but hoped that there might be a way in. She was suddenly aware of her hunger and thirst. It was a hot day and she wanted to get out of the sun and clean up.

They left the driveway and walked along a newly laid cream-colored interlocking path by the side of the cottage that led into the back garden. The garden was large and surrounded by flowers, trees, bushes and plants of all types. There was a fishpond off to the left corner of a flat and emerald green manicured lawn. A small patio with a closed green canvas umbrella, table and chairs was in front of the back door.

"You try the door. I'll try the windows," Monika directed.

Jesse crossed over to the door and Monika went to the first of three windows that were equally spaced apart along the rear of the cottage adjacent to the back door. She imagined that they were the windows of the bedrooms of the cottage.

Jesse, as expected, found a locked door. He turned to check on Monika's progress. She had tried the first window and was now trying the second.

"Over here. I think it isn't locked," she called to him as she checked the frame. She pried at the small window and sure enough it slid up and open. "I'll go in and unlock the door." It had been a bit of luck, the first good thing that had happened in the past couple of days. Monika took it as a sign of things to come.

She jumped onto the sill and pulled herself into the room behind the window. Inside was a bedroom decorated in the colonial style with a large dresser against one wall and a comfy looking bed on the other. She landed on the carpeted floor in-between them and made her way to the bedroom door. The light from the outside brightly illuminated the inside of the house.

She went from the bedroom down a short hall that led to a remodeled modern kitchen and the back door. The cottage was bright and cheery. She crossed to the back door and unlocked it. Jesse opened it and came in.

"This is nice," he remarked at the first class appearance of the interior. "These people are wealthy?" he asked and stated at the same time.

"Yeah. They're comfortable." Monika felt awkward and changed the subject. "Why don't you go and clean up. There are probably some clothes here that will fit. I'll get us some food and call James."

"Oh. Sorry. I 'spose I am a mess." Jesse became aware of his soiled clothes. "I'll go find the...ah..." There was an awkwardness between them. Jesse walked out of the kitchen in search of clothes and the washroom.

Monika opened the fridge door. It was not very full. It contained only some unopened canned juices. Obviously James' parents were going to stock-up on their arrival on Friday. She went to the cupboard next to the fridge and began to search through them. She found some canned stew and canned fruit. She put them on the counter and seeing the can opener, preceded to open them. She found a couple of bowls and poured the contents of the cans into them. There was a large microwave on the counter next to the fridge. She put the stew in the microwave and turned it on. She was very hungry.

On the wall next to the fridge by the hall entrance, a cream-colored phone was attached to the wall. Monika crossed to the phone and picked up the receiver. She punched in a number and held the phone to her ear. After several seconds the phone connected and started to ring at the other end.

"Federal Building," a receptionist answered.

"James Anstey please." Monika felt weak kneed.

"I'll connect you to his office. One moment, please." The phone rang again.

"Investigations. How can I help you?" another woman answered.

"James Anstey, please."

"I'm sorry but he's left for the day. Can I help."

"No." Monika was disappointed. Why wasn't James at work?

"Can I take a message?"

"No. Ah yes. Could you tell him Monika called and that I'll call him later?"

"I sure can."

"Thank you." Monika hung the phone back on its wall mount. "Why would he have left early?" she wondered.

Picking up the phone, she punched in another

number. After several rings the phone was answered. She had dialed James' cellular phone and it had transferred to his home number. She was disappointed and wondered why he hadn't answered his cell phone. He always carried it with him.

"Hi." It was James' voice. "After the tone leave me a message and phone number. I'll call you back." There was a beep.

"James. Where are you? I need to talk to you. It's urgent. It's about the President." Monika wasn't sure how long she and Jesse would be at his parents, so she didn't leave a number. "I'll try you again later." She hung up.

James' home answering service was attached to his computer. He had it programmed to forward all his messages immediately to his cellular phone. There was no need for Monika to make two calls.

- - - - - - - - - - - - - - -

After Jesse was finished, he had called out to Monika from down the hall as he exited the bathroom and went into one of the rooms. He had found some clothes and would change into them. Monika, upon hearing the all clear, went down the hall into the bathroom.

The cottage had a simple layout. There was the kitchen at the back and a hall that led to the three rooms. There was a 'L' junction at the far end of the hall past the bedroom door through which

Monika had first entered the cottage. It led into the front living room about twenty-five feet away from the kitchen. The three bedrooms were at the back of the cottage and off the south side of the hall. There was one single door on the north side, leading to the bathroom, about twelve feet away from the kitchen.

Everything in the cottage reflected the care and wealth of its owners. It was carpeted throughout in a light green broadloom. There were all sorts of arts and crafts, books, oil and watercolor paintings and knickknacks, stylishly displayed in the rooms and hall. It had been remodeled with taste. Monika sensed that she would like James' parents.

Monika quietly locked the bathroom door and took a shower. She did not want to offend Jesse by locking the door, but she really didn't know him and with all that had happened to her recently, she didn't want to take any chances. It gave her a more secure feeling.

When she was done, she exited the bathroom and went into one of the other bedrooms. In that room she found some clean clothes—a pair of blue jeans and a man's white cotton shirt. They were a little large, but looked good on her. There was a phone in the room on a table next to a small bed. She picked it up. She would try James again. She expected to get him this time. The phone rang several times and then was answered again by his service. This time she left a message telling him where she was. Hopefully he would call back soon. After she finished the call she put the receiver down and left the room. She did not notice in her agitation that she had not put the receiver properly in its cradle. The phone line was still open.

- - - - - - - - - - - - - - -

Both Monika and Jesse were seated at the kitchen table of James' parent's cottage. They had both cleaned-up and found fresh clothes. They had eaten the stew and were discussing what they should do next.

"What's wrong?" Jesse noticed Monika's stare.

"Sorry, but it's amazing what they've done. I mean, the other Jess in Key Largo is exactly like you. Sorry. You probably don't want to hear that but it is spooky. I feel like you should know me better."

Jesse had found a razor in the bathroom and shaven off his beard. Clean-shaven, he was now an exact duplicate of the other clones.

"I know. It's scary, but I am the real one."

"I know. It's just…"

"What about your fiancé?" Jesse changed the subject.

"I've tried calling, but he's not at work or home."

"So what are we going to do?"

"We'll have to get to Jefferson ourselves somehow and stop them."

"With all the Secret Service there? It will be impossible to get anywhere near the island."

"No. I thought about that. I know all the security forces will be on the island, but the media won't start arriving until tomorrow. We could go to the main Key West dock…"

"Mallory Lock. It's at the end of Duval." Jesse helped her. This was the main tourist dock, where all the cruise ships moored. There would be an array of boats for hire there.

"And get on board with one of the crews."

"That won't be easy."

"I know, but I'll figure something out. We'll find a way."

"Supposing we're successful and we get on a boat. Then what?"

"Well…" Monika wasn't entirely sure. She was making it up as she went. "Get to Jefferson. Find the clone and switch you with him. Then we try to save the President by stopping them from switching him with his clone."

"That will save him on Friday, but it won't stop them from trying again, or coming after us. We're the only ones that know about them."

"We'll have to expose them."

They both fell silent. It would be a difficult task.

"No. What we have to do is find the clone. Switch places with him and go through with their plan. We have to catch them in the act. It's the only way to get them all."

"What?"

"Hear me out. If we can get to the island without being spotted and locate the clone, I can go through with the dive. I know where it's taking place. I don't know their plan, but I can go through with the original itinerary. Hopefully that will be enough. If it isn't, then the President and I will have a nice swim. When we resurface, I'll tell him what's going on. If it is, I'll go along with it and protect the President."

"What about me?"

"You stay around the fort in case something goes wrong and keep an eye on the Major and his men."

"So first thing in the morning we should leave." Monika agreed with the plan, unless James returned her call by then. There was no other choice.

"Early. Before dawn." Jesse confirmed.

"Then we'd better get some rest."

Chapter 10

It had been a long thirty-six hours since his arrival in Key Largo. Not one clue had surfaced to lead him to her.

James had spent the whole day on Wednesday with detective Swan. They had both re-questioned all the staff at the Sandy Reef and followed up even the remotest of discrepancies. The longest interrogation was with the Room Service employee who had delivered the meal on the evening that Monika disappeared, but nothing came from it. Monika had been abducted without a trace.

James had checked with his office several times during that day, but there was nothing. He had brought his cell phone with him, but had neglected to bring the charger for the battery. The phone had gone dead and he had no way of recharging it. He was angry with himself for not having the charger with him, but he hadn't expected this last minute excursion. If Monika tried to call she wouldn't get through. She would be bounced to his answering service.

It had been a long and arduous day of questioning and re-questioning. He and Swan had again gone through Monika's cabin and still turned up nothing. She had vanished into thin air. There was little that could be done. By late in the evening Swan had left James on his own at the Sandy Reef. He had other investigations and paperwork to catch up on.

James had decided to stay at the Sandy Reef until Saturday morning. He felt that he had to remain there. It made him feel better to be in the place where Monika had last been. He would go to Key West as planned on Saturday. Maybe she would show up at the airport. It was a long shot, but it was the only hope that he had to hold on to and no matter how foolish he professionally knew it was, he wasn't emotionally willing to let it go.

Having had a late dinner, James retired to his room. Everyone at the resort was being extremely kind to him, but he needed to be alone. Something was gnawing away at him. He knew that Monika was alive, but he could not sense where she was. He felt impotent.

He turned on his TV to add distraction to his

thoughts. The room was small, but cozy. It was on the second story of the resort and looked out over the grounds of the resort to the ocean. It was dark out. He stood mesmerized in front of the window staring out into the night. He looked at his watch: 10:30 PM. He moved away from the window. He didn't draw the curtains. He turned and walked over to the bed, plunked himself down and stared at the ceiling. He wondered where Monika was. It had been a tumultuous couple of days. He closed his eyes to rest a moment. Without realizing it, he fell asleep.

- - - - - - - - - - - - - - -

Suddenly James awoke to the hissing static noise of the TV. He was startled and sat up. He had not intended to fall asleep. He reached for the TV remote and turned it off. The room was quiet. He checked the time on his wristwatch. It was 3:30 Thursday morning. He felt groggy and uneasy. Something inside told him to check his messages at home. He stretched over to the phone on the bedside table, picked up the handset, dialed an outside line and punched in his number. He lay back on the bed. The phone rang two times and his voice announcement began.

"Hi. After the..." He pressed a key and the computer, stopping his outgoing message, went into its remote message retrieval mode.

"Please enter your password."

James entered his password from the phone

keypad.

"You have…two…new messages. To play…"

James knew what to do. He didn't wait for the announcement to finish. He pressed the required keys to hear the message.

"James. Where are you? I need to talk to you. It's urgent. It's about the Pres… I'll try you again later." Monika's voice became distorted on the playback and the word was not clear.

James' heart skipped a beat. She was alive! He chastised himself for falling asleep and not checking his messages earlier.

"If you have finished listening to this…" the automated voice continued.

James pushed several more keys to save and then repeat the current message.

"James. Where are you? I need to talk to you. It's urgent. It's about the President. I'll try you again later." It played again.

Monika's voice seemed distressed, but she was alive. He was overjoyed.

"To hear the next message press…" the automated voice went through its routine.

James was now standing as he pushed the required keys.

"James. I'm in Key West at your parent's. Please call. I need you."

James disconnected from the call. Not only was Monika alive, she was safe at his parent's place. He was so excited. He began to place a call to Key

West. He dialed the number twice, having fumbled the first time on the keypad. The line finally connected. There was a busy tone. She was there!

James was ecstatic. He put the phone down and jumped up from his bed. He would try again in a few minutes. He paced the room and checked his watch several times as he paced.

After a couple of minutes he dialed again, but the phone was still busy. He hung up and dialed the operator.

"Bell South."

"Yes. Could you check the last call for me please, the line's always busy."

"Just one moment sir." The operator went offline. After several moments she returned. "There's no one on the line sir. Would you like to report the problem?"

"No. Thank you." James disconnected. He contemplated what he should do. There was something wrong, but now he knew where to start.

He went through his pockets and pulled out detective Swan's card. He read Swan's home number and punched it quickly into the keypad. The phone rang.

"Hello." Swan awakened from sleep.

"Dan. She's alive!" James voice showed his pleasure. "I think I know where she is."

"Slow down. Slow down." The detective was surprised by the time of the call and its content. "How?"

"She's left a message on my machine at home. She's at my parent's place in Key West."

"Is she okay?"

"I don't know. I can't get through."

"You stay there." Detective Swan threw his sheets back. "I'll be right over."

- - - - - - - - - - - - - - -

By the time Detective Swan arrived at the Sandy Reef, James was waiting, briefcase in hand, in the lobby. He had freshened up and shaved.

"Are you ready?" Swan greeted James.

"Yes."

"Then let's go. I'll drive."

"How long will it take?"

"It's usually a couple of hours, but at this time of morning we can do it in a lot less."

They both hurried out from the lobby. Dan's car was parked in front. They got in and pulled away.

"How did she sound?' Dan asked as he turned onto the highway heading south. There was no one else on the road. An eerie silence permeated the pre-dawn hours.

"A little stressed, but otherwise all right."

"How do you think she got there?"

"I don't know. She mentioned something about the President. I'm glad she's safe."

"What about the President?"

"She didn't say."

"We'll know soon enough."

Detective Swan pushed the accelerator. He wasn't concerned with the speed limit. They were both in a hurry to get to Key West. The fact that the phone was not working meant trouble. Neither of them mentioned their understanding of this fact. They hoped when they got there they would find Monika alive and well.

Chapter 11

At five o'clock the next morning, Monika and Jesse left the cottage and were got into the pick-up. It was just beginning to get light. Monika wondered why James hadn't called her. She couldn't understand what had happened to him. It was so unlike him not to return her call almost immediately. Since he had not called, she and Jesse had no choice but to follow their plan. They were on their own.

"So are you okay with all this?" Jesse started the truck and asked before he backed out of the driveway.

"Yeah. Just a little nervous."

"Me too. But we'll be okay."

He backed out onto Whitehead and drove west.

No one else in the neighborhood was up and the street was quiet. Other than the few sprinklers watering some of the properties they passed, there was no other activity. There was a freshness and a warmth to air. It was going to be another hot day. Already the temperature felt like it was in the high sixties.

Monika gazed out her window marveling at the floral growth and wondering what had happened to James. If she had the chance, she would like to spend more time in Key West and explore everything with him.

They soon traveled the full length of Whitehead and came to an intersection. Jesse signaled and turned right. There was more activity here, in large part due to the Presidential visit. They drove a short distance and turned left onto Duval Street.

"What's this street?" Monika was fascinated by the quaintness of the area. It reminded her of Provincetown in Cape Cod, Massachusetts, with its cute clapboard houses. Like Cape Cod, this was obviously a tourist area. All the houses were in pristine condition painted in whites, yellows, and light blues. Ornate second floor verandas fronted many of the reconditioned houses that now housed businesses aimed at the tourist trade.

"Duval Street. The longest street in the world. It's the main draw here." Jesse acted as tour guide.

"It's pretty." Monika admired the sights as they

drove. After a couple of minutes, Jesse slowed down.

"There it is. Mallory Square. That's where the media will head out from." Jesse pointed ahead.

The area was bustling with activity. As they drove up they saw the huge lot to their left almost full of parked cars. To their right were more parked cars and vans with the various logos of the news media. Farther along were a couple of buildings adjacent to the dock that jutted out on a tiny piece of land into the ocean. Between these buildings and parking lots was a protected manmade harbor.

The media had arrived in force. People were scurrying back and forth carrying boxes of the equipment they would need for the event on Jefferson. Some were obviously behind-the-scenes crew, dressed very casually, and others were on-air personalities who were dressed more business-like. About a dozen day-tour boats were moored along the enclosed harbor. There were people on the boats getting ready to leave and others just arriving and loading up.

"We'll park over there." Jesse indicated a vacant spot in front of several large gasoline storage tanks to the far left of the harbor near the ocean side.

Seeing the crowd of people, Monika realized how difficult it was going to be to get aboard one of the boats unnoticed. It appeared that each of the major media crews had their own boats that they had chartered. They would all know each other. Monika needed to find a way to get aboard one of the boats.

Driving carefully through the hoard of people, Jesse parked the pick-up.

"Let's get out and walk around. Maybe we can figure something out." He was also at a loss as to how to get on one of the boats unnoticed. He waited a moment with Monika in the pick-up before they got out into the hustle and bustle of the crowd.

"Okay," Monika agreed.

They got out and began to walk amongst the people. They slowly made their way toward the boats on the southeast side of the dock. They stayed close together and tried to avoid bumping into the crews that were self-importantly hurrying about oblivious to anyone around them. Monika sensed that this was not the normal type of crowd she was used to. This was much wilder, a hectic frenzy of egocentric showbiz prima donnas.

Monika managed to lead the way and soon she and Jesse were standing in front of one of the larger moored boats. On its transom was written in large black letters: REPUBLICAN QUEEN, centered under it in smaller print was: Key West.

"What now?" Jesse asked. They stood amongst the crowd in front of the large boat facing each other.

"I don't know. I'll think of something. There's got to be…"

"Monika? Monika Queller?" a voice called out from the boat.

Monika turned round to see who was calling her. Jesse stayed behind her.

"Monika?" Up on the main deck of the two-deck boat a petite woman dressed in a mauve business outfit, with shoulder length teased hair, was waving down to her. "Monika. It's me. Over here."

"Carolynn?" Monika identified her old Stanford roommate. "What are you doing here?"

"Meet me at the gangplank." She indicated that Monika should go down to the stern of the boat where a short gangplank bridged the boat to shore.

"Come on. Follow my lead. I think this is our ride," Monika quickly whispered to Jesse as she waved back to Carolynn who was making her way along the deck.

Monika and Jesse pushed their way to the back of the boat just as Carolynn came to the gangplank.

"Ooooh," Carolynn threw open her arms and started down the gangplank. She came onto the shore. Monika opened her arms. They hugged.

"I haven't heard from you in so long. What have you been up to?" Carolynn was overjoyed to bump into Monika.

"Oh this and that. I'm engaged." Monika always liked Carolynn. She was full of spunk.

"Engaged? Whew! I don't believe it. Man-eater Queller?!"

"Here, look." Monika pulled back and offered her left hand. Upon it was James' ring.

"Now that's a rock. Is he rich? Does he have a brother, or even a sister?" She giggled and embraced Monika again.

"What about you?" Monika asked.

"Married to the job. I'm a reporter at WCBC in Atlanta," she jokingly lowered her voice and imitated a Walter Cronkite type voice. They both laughed.

"That's great." Monika was truly happy to see her.

"Why are you here?"

"Oh. I'm covering the Presidential visit." Monika, seeing her opportunity, began to weave her story. She did not like lying to Carolynn, but it was safer that way. She didn't want to involve her in something dangerous. After it was all over, if it worked out, she could explain everything. Maybe even give Carolynn the exclusive to the story.

"Really?" Carolynn was doubly surprised.

"Yes. This is my cameraman." She turned to introduce Jesse. "Jesse. Carolynn. Carolynn, Jesse."

"Hi." Jesse stepped forward and shook

Carolynn's hand and stepped back.

"Hi." Carolynn was suspicious. "Where's your gear?" she asked of Jesse.

"Oh. We're on that boat with…" Monika interrupted and turned to see and point at a boat that was moored farther down. "The FOXX group. Over there. All our stuff's on board." She had saved Jesse from having to answer. Jesse just smiled and acknowledged Monika's story.

"FOXX. Not bad." Carolynn was impressed.

"No I'm not with FOXX. We work with a local cable show, out of Key Largo."

"Conch Cable." Jesse joined in and added his part to the tale.

"We're sharing a ride with them." Monika smiled at Jesse to thank him.

"Hey. Why don't you continue that onboard, ladies? We're trying to get some work done here." A group of guys who were blocked from the boat by Monika and Carolynn's gangplank reunion, complained.

"Oh. I'm sorry," Carolynn spoke out to them with disdain and then turned to Monika. "Come with me."

"What?" Monika feigned misunderstanding.

"I want to catch up with you. Come to Jefferson on this boat. We'll have a few hours to talk. It will be so boring without you."

"Well…" she looked at Jesse and then back to Carolynn. "Sure. That'd be great."

"Come on ladies. Let's go. Move it or lose it."
The men were out of patience.

"Come on." Carolynn led the way. Monika and
Jesse followed. "I'll get you some press passes,
then nobody will bother us," she offered.

They walked across the short gangplank onto
the boat.

"Hey George," Carolynn called out to a stocky
man who was talking to another man on the deck.
"Get me a couple of press passes. My friends are
coming with us. They're okay." She turned back
to Monika and Jesse. "There's a bar on the upper
deck. Let's go up there."

"Okay. We'd better move out of the way."
Monika looked around and noticed that where
they were standing on deck was in the way of
other passengers who were trying to move along
the boat.

The boat was a large eighty-foot day cruiser. It
was a modern craft painted white. It resembled a
mini ocean liner instead of a small pleasure yacht.
It had a lower, main and two upper decks. On the
lower deck was the dining area from which its
patrons could see out to the ocean through large
windows that ran the length of the room, along
the ship's hull. On the main deck, which they
were now on, a narrow gangway with a wooden
railing ran the perimeter of the ship, allowing the
passengers to access either the poop deck at the
stern on the level above, or the large open area at

the front of the boat. There was an exposed white
metal set of stairs half way up the boat along the
gangway that led to the upper decks. Another
staircase was similarly located on the port side.
The boat was usually rented out for three-hour
dinner tours, but today it was acting as a ferry and
a floating hotel.

The sun was now up and the morning was bright
and warm. The three made their way to the stair-
way and climbed to the next deck. The second
deck was smaller than the dining room below.
They continued up to the third deck, which was
on top of the boat and open to the elements. It was
situated behind the ship's large forward smokestack and bridge. A small blue canvas awning
covered part of the deck. There were tables and
chairs scattered throughout the twenty by twenty-
foot space. A bar with a crowd of people trying to
place orders for an early morning coffee, was at
the end under the smokestack. There was a railing
several feet beyond the canvas enclosure along
the circumference of the other three sides. The
panoramic view of the harbor, Key West and the
ocean from this thirty-foot high vantagepoint was
fabulous. They crossed to an empty table on the
starboard side and sat down overlooking the
activity of Mallory Square and the harbor. The
sun was bright and the day was getting warmer.
Monika used her hand as a sun visor.

As they sat down, Carolynn's assistant George

came over to them with two press passes. He handed them to Carolynn without saying a word then turned to leave.

"Thanks George. Get me a couple of ball-caps as well." Carolynn said. He barely acknowledged her order as he scurried away. Carolynn had noticed Monika's discomfort and knew that the ball caps would help.

"He's part of the set up crew and my part-time assistant. He doesn't like me. Imagine that." She felt that she had to explain his unusual behavior. Being part of the set-up crew was all the explanation that Carolynn thought was needed amongst others of her profession.

"See." Monika played along and lectured Jesse as if to teach an apprentice the ins and outs of the industry.

"Here you go." Carolynn handed the passes to her guests. "Now no one will bother you."

"Thanks. The hats will be nice. We left ours on the boat."

"That's okay. You can give me one of yours when we get to Jefferson. We can swap."

A loud blast of the ship's horn sounded and they all jumped. There was the sound of the gangplank being stowed and the shouts of the boat's crew as they cast off the lines. They were about to set out to Ft. Jefferson.

Monika and Jesse put on their passes. They had made it on board and were now en route to the fort. The dangerous part of their plan was about to unfold. By mid-afternoon they would be at the island. They would have to act quickly to find Jess and make the switch without being discovered. Monika's heart went cold at the thought of what might be ahead. She wished James was here. She hoped she would see him again soon.

Chapter 12

Dan was an excellent driver. They had had an uneventful trip through the Keys. The pre-dawn light on the ocean as they drove along the causeway from key to key was a sight that James had never seen. Though his parents had had a place in Key West for years, he had always flown in to them and never driven the route from Key Largo down. The beauty and the vastness of the ocean with the horizon on all sides of you, broken only by the thin strip of gray highway elevated a few feet from the water and the occasional key, was almost indescribable. Though physically unique, it was much more of an emotional experience than a visual one.

Around 5:30 AM Dan and James pulled up into

the driveway of James' parent's cottage. It did not appear that anyone was home.

"This is a nice place." Dan commented as they got out of the car.

"Yeah. They've done a lot with it over the years. It's really very peaceful here. You wouldn't know you were in the middle of a busy street. I'll try the front. You go 'round back." James went into his trained CIA mode when in an uncertain situation. The place seemed too quiet to him and he wasn't sure what to expect.

"Okay." Dan carefully made his way along the driveway and disappeared along the side of the cottage.

James went up the main walkway to the front door. The front yard of the cottage reminded one of a thatched cottage in a fairly tale. It was full of vegetation and flowers and a lawn so green and perfect that you felt like you were not in the real world. The whole garden was laid out with gentle curves, everything running into and compliment-ing each other.

The cottage had a low sloping roof, which over-hung a five-foot verandah that ran the length of it. Two large picture windows separated the garden from the living room inside. Two chairs, made out of woven and bent branch twigs, stood on the rust colored ceramic brick floor of the verandah. A low black wrought iron balustrade skirted the verandah.

The walls of the cottage were composed of hand split three-quarter inch thick California redwood cedar shingles, placed in uneven rows ten or so inches apart. The shingles had unevenly weathered, giving the cottage a natural look that fit in with the garden. The front door was painted a dark forest green and had antiqued brass fittings.

James went up to and quietly tried the door. It was locked. He bent down to the thick tan-colored grass mat that lay at the threshold of the door upon the red tiles and lifted the corner. There was a key hidden beneath it. He picked it up, placed it into the keyhole of the handle and turned. The door unlocked.

Dan had made his way around the back and, keeping an eye out for any occupants, had tried the patio door of the kitchen. It was locked. He tried each window but they were also locked tight. There was no entry into the cottage from the back and there was no sign that anyone had forced entry. He returned along the side of the house to the front to see how James had fared.

James slowly opened the door and entered the cottage. It was not too dark. The sun had risen and was beginning to find its way through the trees to the house, but even in the half-light he knew the layout well. No one was in the living room. He carefully made his way across to the hall. He came to each door along the hall and listened before he slowly opened each door. Though not completely bright, there was enough outside early dawn light to see.

In the first room the bed was all messed up, but there was no one to be seen. The second room was untouched, and the third was in a similar condition to the first. He checked the bathroom. It had been recently used. The counter area around the sink was wet and there were soiled towels on the floor. He continued to the kitchen feeling certain that, whoever was here, would be in there.

Dan came back around the front of the cottage and saw the open door, but not James. He drew his gun from his side belt, raised it in front of him, and entered.

James stopped in the hall just before entering the kitchen. There was a small glow coming from the florescent light of the oven. He took in a breath and then burst into the room. There was nobody there, but there was evidence that someone had been—and recently. On the kitchen table were a couple of dirty plates and glasses. James felt let down. He had hoped to find her here.

The noise of something falling and breaking on the floor pierced the silence of the cottage. James ran to the kitchen door and concealed himself from view. He heard someone coming down the hall. He held his breath and readied himself to attack if necessary. Dan came into the kitchen.

"Oh there you are," he said as James, recognizing the intruder, came out of his concealment. He holstered his gun.

"Nobody's here." James sounded disappointed.

"I didn't think so. Let's put on some light. Sorry I think I broke something in there." Dan found the light switch and turned on the kitchen lights.

The added light clearly revealed a kitchen that had recently been used. There were two plates and glasses on the kitchen table, and opened cans in the sink. James went over to the cans, picked them up and examined them.

"It looks like they were here not long ago." James determined by the freshness of the leftover food along the inside of the cans.

"Let's give the place a thorough search. I'll take the living room. There's got to be something here." Dan started back down the hall. There was no time to waste. Monika might still be nearby. If they hurried they might be able to figure out what happened and help her.

- - - - - - - - - - - - - - - -

James and Dan had made a quick search of the cottage and rejoined each other at the kitchen table where they compared notes. It was six in the morning. It was getting brighter outside. The sun was rising higher in the sky.

"So you think there were two of them here?" Dan questioned.

"Yes. Monika and a man. There's a man's dirty clothing in the first room. He's fairly large. Monika's jeans and Stanford sweatshirt are in the other. They're also dirty, smelly and heavily soiled."

"So they've both been through the same hardship?"

"Yeah. I think so. I don't think that this man is holding her captive, but that they are somehow in this together."

"Yeah, but what? Why wouldn't they remain here?"

"It has to be something big and dangerous to make them leave so soon. They were here about an hour ago."

"So they're still in the area?"

"Maybe. I found the phone off the hook in one of the rooms. That's why I couldn't get through. Probably an oversight."

"So when she didn't hear from you, she decided that she couldn't stay? But why?"

"I don't know. She said it was about the President, but I don't see how. They were sure in a hurry. They left everything thrown about."

"But if they were here together, why not go to the police?"

"I don't know."

"Maybe she's still captive and the guy is her kidnapper. Maybe he's nervous and didn't want to hang around."

"Yeah, but where would they go? Why would the kidnapper be on the run? Why would Monika call if she was still captive? How is the President involved? Why would they come here? Surely the kidnapper would have a hideout of his own and other plans."

"Yeah. That seems reasonable. So he's not a kidnapper. What is he then?"

"I don't know, but I know Monika, and something is up or she would still be here."

They both fell silent in contemplation of the mystery.

"Is there anything out of the ordinary going on down here?" James asked.

"Just the Presidential visit, but that's seventy miles away at Ft. Jefferson."

"The President is coming here? When?"

"Friday."

"Anything else? Any other stops?"

"No. That's all."

"Maybe it has something to do with the visit?"

"Yeah, but what?"

"I don't know. But there has to be something."

"So what do you want to do?" Dan wasn't sure about their next steps.

James rubbed his right hand over his chin. He had a strange feeling stirring within that he could not quite figure out. There was much more to all this than met the eye. There was something he was missing. He wondered where Monika was and what she was involved in. There was only one obvious possibility.

"I think Monika has stumbled onto something,

something about the President's visit and she doesn't know who to trust. That's why she called me. Is there any way we can get to Ft. Jefferson before Friday?"

"You think it has to do with the visit?" Dan was startled. He would never have made the connection.

"Maybe not, but it's our only lead, and I don't want to sit around here and wait."

Chapter 13

Construction on Ft. Jefferson began in 1846 and continued for a period of thirty years. Though it was never completed, its six-sided, forty-five foot high and eight-foot thick masonry walls still stood as a testament to man's ability to prevail against nature. The fort, built to protect the continental United States from invasion from the south, was surrounded by a break-water moat and housed six gun turret towers. It was truly a remarkable historic sight. Also know as 'The Gibraltar of the Caribbean', it brought the turbulent eighteenth century world of politics into the otherwise peaceful Dry Tortugas islands. Ironically, the fort was obsolete before it could be finished. It was man's progress and not the power of nature that in the end it succumbed to.

Major Britin and his men had arrived on Wednesday to set up a makeshift camp on the north shore of the island on the only bit of land outside the fort's walls with enough space to house them. Along with the Secret Service, they had been making preparations for the Presidential visit. Everything had been done with the efficiency of the military. The usually unkempt deserted fort had been spruced up. It proudly came alive and exuded some of its previous glory.

Below the main arched interior hallways that ran the mile perimeter of the fort, was the sub level. It was here that the men who had been garrisoned in the past had lived and kept their provisions. In the southernmost section of the fort, Britin's men had set-up an infirmary. Major Britin was standing in the infirmary making final arrangements with Dr. Pearl. Unbeknownst to either of them, one of the doctor's ancestors, Dr. Samuel Mudd had been incarcerated here in the late 1860s when the fort was used as a prison, after allegedly setting John Wilkes Booth's broken leg. He had also used this room as an infirmary. Other than these ghosts, the two men were alone.

"We're all set. Is everything in place?" the Major asked. The room was full of medical supplies and equipment that lay waiting in case of an emergency. Several large locked stainless steel canisters were placed side by side along the eastern wall. The noise of a small generator forced the men to talk loudly. Several halogen lights placed on stands in the corners of the tiny eight by fifteen-foot room illuminated the space well.

"Yes. The equipment is ready and working. We should have enough power to complete the procedure." Dr. Pearl had been worried that the two generators they had brought might not survive the damp four-hour boat trip to get here, but they had and were now operating. There was no power or any other supplies on the island. Everything had to be brought, including food and drinking water. "I'll set everything up after the President has changed into his dive gear. It won't take long. I only have to unlock the canisters and plug the equipment in. It should only take five minutes to be up and fully operational."

"What about the drain."

"It's still intact. I had one of the men go down and check it out. It runs straight out into the moat on the other side of the wall. There shouldn't be a problem. We can make the switch easily."

"And the clone?"

The doctor walked over to one of the larger stainless steel canisters. "In here, asleep. I'll inject the serum into him after we've uploaded the President's memory. He'll be unconscious for about an hour afterwards, but no one will suspect a thing. We can put the President back into the canister and ship him out with the rest of the equipment."

"Will he survive in there?"

"Yes. The drug I'm using slows down his heart rate. He'll be in a death-like state until we get back to the base. There's plenty of air inside to last."

"Good." Major Britin was pleased that the plan was proceeding without glitches. He was looking out to the moat and the ocean beyond through an eighteen-inch arched opening in the infirmary's wall. There was no glass in the opening and a warm sea breeze blew against his face. "I'm posting two men outside. No one will be allowed to enter this area." He raised his left hand and regarded his watch. "I've got a meeting with the Secret Service. Good luck doctor." He left the infirmary.

On the level above the infirmary, the Secret Service had set up a command center overlooking the area of the moat where the President would make his dive. Inside the fortified walls the air was cool and damp. An eight-foot wide area was cluttered with a large portable table, chairs, and other equipment. There were several men seated around the table waiting for a meeting to begin.

"Ah, Major Britin you're just in time. We're about to begin." Agent Gorman greeted him. Gorman was a twenty-year veteran of the service. His dark short hair was graying around the temples, and topped off the air of competency that emanated from his tall, sturdy frame. Agent Hemings had hand picked him for this assignment and he was pleased to be in charge. "Please have a seat." He directed Britin to a seat in the front row.

"I want to run through the schedule one last time before the media arrives this afternoon. So pay attention." Agent Gorman spoke loudly to the small group of his Secret Service and Major Britin's men. His voice echoed down the long main promenade of the fort.

"The media arrive at fifteen hundred. There will be ten boats. They will all be moored here," he referred to a large map of the island placed in front of them, "along the coal docks. They will unload their equipment in this area here," he indicated with a pointer a northern section of the fort on the opposite side of their present location. "And here. Some of them want to set up camp on the northwest section of the fort's parade ground and some will remain onboard their charters. They all have passes. Anyone without a pass is to be detained." He paused and checked that the group had understood.

"This evening around nineteen hundred hours, they will come to the northeast parade grounds for an orientation. After that they are free to roam the island. Some will want to get some background footage. They have been told that they may only interview myself or Major Britin. We've set up an area here…" he indicated the walled area due east, "to accommodate them. After midnight, no one will be permitted in the command center area. Here and here." He pointed to the locations on the map.

"On Friday at eleven hundred hours, the President's helicopter, Marine One, will arrive on land inside the fort on the southeast section of the parade grounds. We've cleared an area. Major Britin's men will set-up a perimeter and secure the President's helicopter. No unauthorized personnel will be allowed on the parade grounds until after the President leaves. They must all use the main floor promenade. They will be allowed to film, but not to interview the President."

"The President will be brought here at 11:15 for a small ceremony where he will unveil a plaque on the wall about twenty feet from here down the promenade."

"Sir." One of Gorman's men had a question.

"Yes Bill."

"What about the First Lady? Is she on this trip?"

"Good question. No. She's staying behind in Key West. The President will join her after his visit here. Any other questions?" He waited before continuing.

"At 11:30 the President will go down to the storage area here and get ready for his dive. Captain Ehrlich will be with the President from that point until after the dive."

"At 12:00 Captain Ehrlich and the President will come back to the main level and exit to the moat. We've constructed a temporary set of stairs from the large opening there." He pointed down the promenade. About ten feet away was an opening in the masonry that faced out to the moat and ocean.

"Now most of you will be stationed on the breakwater around the moat where Captain Ehrlich and the President will make their dive. A couple of you will be watching from the fort.

"At 12:10 the Captain and the President will be in the water. We're going to put two of you about thirty feet away in the water on standby, but you are not to dive with the President. The President has requested that you stand down, and we think on this occasion it will be okay. The moat is a protected water and there should be no danger. Your job is to standby in case of emergency. Captain Ehrlich should be able to handle the underwater event alone. It's what the President wants. Now, we've already done our preliminary dives in the moat and everything has been checked out. No one is allowed to enter the moat until after the dive with Captain Ehrlich.

"At 12:40 Captain Ehrlich and the President will resurface. At 12:45 they will come back into the fort and the President will go back to the storage area to change."

"Who will be guarding the President in the sub level?" Bill asked.

"Major Britin's men are in charge of the security in and around the infirmary, storage room and command center sub level. We will be stationed outside the fort.

"At 13:00 hours," Agent Gorman continued, "the President will return to the main level and leave for Marine One."

"13:10 is 'wheels up' and he will be in the air and our job is done. Any other questions?" Wheels up was the Secret Service code for take off of Marine One.

There was general chatting amongst the assembled group, but no questions ensued.

"Okay. Captain Ehrlich, would you mind staying behind a moment after everyone leaves?" he said to Jess and received a visual acknowledgment. "Okay gentlemen. It's time to work. Dismissed."

The group got up from their chairs and began to disperse. Major Britin stood on the opposite side of the promenade watching. Jess came forward. He and Agent Gorman stood in front of the large table alone.

"Captain Ehrlich. I understand you've dived with the President before."

"Yes Sir. In Key Largo. He and the First Lady came to the reef park."

"That was before he was President wasn't it?"

"Yes Sir."

"You've got an important duty here. He's the President now and we don't take any risks. Understand?"

"Yes, Sir. It's going to be a very straightforward dive. The moat's protected from the open ocean. There won't be any problems."

"Good. Then you'd better get back to your duties."

"Thank you, Sir." Jess turned and walked away from the table.

"Captain Ehrlich," Major Britin called out to Jess as he walked away, "Let me walk with you."

Britin hurried after Jess.

Chapter 14

Monika and Carolynn had had a long visit. Jesse was tired of their non-stop chatter. He was relieved when Garden Key and Ft. Jefferson finally came into sight across the flat blue ocean.

"There it is," he announced.

The three of them had remained sitting on the upper deck for the whole journey. He was grateful to have been given the ball-cap.

"Wow. That's really something. I had no idea it was so vast." Monika was impressed.

"Yeah. It's something else. To think it was never really used other than for minor things. It's a bit of an albatross." Carolynn interjected.

"It looks like an old European fortress, like in

the Count of Monte Cristo, but only fifty times bigger. It's amazing that they could have carried all those bricks out here."

"Especially in the eighteen hundreds," Carolynn concurred.

"It was used mostly during the Civil War and World War II, but other than that it's been vacant." Jesse knew the fort well. He had always found Jefferson a fascinating historical monument. Coupled with the stories of pirates and sunken treasure in the Tortugas the fort, with its castle-like facade, added a romanticism to the Florida Keys.

"It's beautiful here." Monika was enjoying the view.

The Caribbean waters surrounding the island were turquoise and mirror flat. It was very inviting. There were many boats out on the water around the fort. It was probably the most activity the old fort had seen in many decades, and probably the most it would see for some time.

"Here Monika. Try these." Carolynn handed her a pair of binoculars that she pulled from her bag.

"Thanks." Monika took them and put them to her eyes. She focused on the fort ahead.

There was a docking area outside the fortified walls with boats moored alongside of it. To the left of the dock was a small recently erected encampment. Men dressed in military clothing were in that area. There was a white sandy beach to the right of the dock and the omnipresent walls of the fort encompassed by a moat. The fortress looked like it rose right on the water. There was no other land that Monika could see, other than the encampment.

Monika turned her attention to the boats on the water. A few of the boats were strategically positioned and anchored upon the water surrounding the fort. On these boats, she could make out what she supposed were Secret Service agents. Together these boats set up a security net around the fort. She wondered if she and Jesse would be able to complete their mission successfully with all the Secret Service and military presence.

"Here. You look." Monika offered the glasses to Jesse.

"No that's okay. Carolynn?" he offered.

"No. You guys keep them. Give them back later. I've got to find my crew. They're probably mad at me for ignoring them on the trip. Why don't you two meet up with me later after the orientation."

"What time is it again?" Monika asked.

"19…" Carolynn tried to convert the hour to the normal time she understood. "Hundred. Ah…7:00 PM. It's all in your itinerary." She began to walk away.

"Okay. See you later then." Monika waved as Carolynn went down the stairs.

"Whew. You guys sure can talk," Jesse said frankly.

"I'm sorry. But she is an old friend and we were lucky that she was here."

"I know. You're right, but…"

"So what do we do next?" Monika abruptly changed the conversation. She wanted his input.

"Once we get ashore, mingle with the crowd, and scout-out the fort. I remember from the briefings that the command center is in the south promenade of the fort. The President is going to dive in the southeast moat. The fort runs in six sections completely around the perimeter of the island. There's a main promenade level inside. Under it is a lower level with rooms and storage areas. "

"What about the clone?"

"Well he's somewhere on the island in the fort around the southeast section with all the equipment. We'll have to split up and find him and make the switch."

"Will we be able to get in there?"

"I think so. We'll use the media connection and try to slip by."

"Then what?"

"Let's wait 'til we get there. Okay?"

"Okay."

They both fell silent in anxious anticipation of what was ahead.

- - - - - - - - - - - - - - -

By three thirty in the afternoon, the REPUBLICAN QUEEN had docked alongside of Ft.

Jefferson. The whole dock area was a swarm of people. Monika and Jesse had disembarked and found it a simple task to get into the fort. There wasn't any security to prevent them from crossing from the dock into the fort. In fact a small crowd of people was already inside talking and setting up equipment.

Now standing inside the main level of the fort's north wall, Monika and Jesse began to walk away from the crowd along the southeastern route of the promenade. They both were wearing their ball-caps low over their eyes. The logo of Caroline's station boldly stood out and they both, with their hats and press passes attached to their shirts, looked like any of the other members of the media.

The promenade had a cement floor and brick arches spaced every fifteen feet, which supported the level above. It resembled a large vault. The brickwork was discolored in places and stained from the salt air. There were large window areas open to the elements situated in every arched section on both sides of the promenade. Some were staggered and others allowed you to view uninterrupted both the ocean and the inner parade ground of the fort. Sets of stairs that led down to the lower level were placed regularly along the promenade. Monika and Jesse carefully made their way along the promenade, which was surprisingly devoid of any security.

"There's nobody here." Monika didn't understand why there wasn't someone on guard duty.

"This is the farthest point from the command center. It's three sections away. There should be someone in the second section of the promenade. It's a big expanse. The whole promenade is about a mile long. They won't place security around all of it until it gets closer to the President's arrival. For now they'll use only a minimum security net close to their command center." Jesse knew all of this from his briefings and past experience in the navy. "But watch out. You never know."

Monika was nervous. She did not know what to expect. She felt butterflies in her stomach. She continued forward listening intently to every sound within the promenade. A cooling breeze was blowing off the ocean into the promenade. She walked on the parade side and Jesse the oceanside. They stayed close to the brick walls and arches just in case someone came along. They continued this way for two sides of the fort without encountering a soul.

- - - - - - - - - - - - - - -

"It's all arranged." Dan hung up the phone in the kitchen. "It wasn't easy, but your office helped. There'll be a boat ready later this afternoon. It's the best I can do. It seems with the President's visit all the boats are chartered. We'll have all the clearances later. It's a four-hour trip. The President arrives at eleven tomorrow."

"That's okay."

"We've got some time to kill. Let's get something to eat. I know a place on the waterfront downtown. Serves the best breakfast around. Interested?"

"I'm not very hungry, but I could use a good coffee."

"Good. Let's go. My treat. We can get some rest when we get back. It's going to be another long day."

They started down the hall and made their way out of the cottage.

- - - - - - - - - - - - - - -

Monika and Jesse were almost through the second section of the fort when they heard footsteps coming in their direction from the third section.

"Hide. Someone's coming," Monika alerted Jesse.

On Jesse's side of the promenade there was a stairwell that led down to the lower level. He hurried onto the stairs and went down out of sight. Monika was farther up the promenade on the right side. The footsteps were getting louder. Just as she was going to make a dash for the steps, two soldiers came around from the gun turret of the third section. They were dressed in fatigues and carried semi-automatic weapons.

"Excuse me, Ma'am," one of the men called out to her, stopping her in mid step. "No one's allowed in this section." The guard saw Monika's press pass. He was under orders to be courteous to the media.

"Oh. I'm glad to see you guys. I'm lost." Monika turned and smiled as she spoke. She put on the helpless woman routine. Jesse was safe and hidden on the stairs.

"What are you looking for?" the same soldier asked, as they both came up to her.

"Ah..." She thought quickly. "Well..." She acted embarrassed. "I'm looking for the ladies."

"You've gone down the wrong section. It's on the northwest side," he became friendlier. He found Monika attractive. The other soldier remained silent, but eyed her up and down.

"Oh, but I was told it was down here." Monika felt uncomfortable, but did not show it.

"No. It's the other way. We'll show you."

"Thank you, but you don't have to..." Monika wanted the soldiers to leave her alone. She wanted to continue her search with Jesse.

"That's no problem, ma'am." The soldier welcomed the chance to spend some time getting to know such a pretty woman. "We're going that way anyway."

"Well, if you're sure. Thanks." Realizing that there was no other option she agreed.

"It's this way, ma'am," the soldier beckoned her. With one soldier on either side, Monika was escorted back up the promenade. She tried to catch a glimpse of Jesse as they passed the stairwell, but could not see him.

Jesse had heard everything that transpired between the soldier and Monika. Now that he and Monika had gotten close to the command center, there would be others on the promenade above. He decided to go down to the lower level and see what was there. He thought he might be able to continue farther on without being discovered.

The stairs were old and made of brick. They were worn and dirty. He felt like he was entering a cave. He followed them straight down about ten feet, to the level below.

At the bottom of the stairs, was a narrow walkway of about four feet in width. It was lit by sunlight that came through small window openings that were about eighteen inches square and built into the walls. The windows were evenly placed along the outer wall facing the moat. It was not a bright place, but Jesse could easily see now that his eyes had adjusted to the dimness of the place. A light breeze was blowing through the walkway from the windows.

Along the left side of the walkway were a series of spaces that had once held doors. Jesse came up to one of the spaces and looked in. It was a small room and must have been used either for storage or accommodations. He stood for a moment and listened. He thought he heard the faint sound of a motor running farther down the walkway. Determined to find the source, he decided to continue on toward it along the walkway.

Carefully he placed his shoes on the crumbling cement floor as he walked. The farther he went the louder the running motor sound became. After two hundred feet the sound had become very loud. It was definitely a motor of some kind. Jesse became more cautious. He realized that he must be approaching the command center and that there would be many more soldiers there. He stared down the long walkway. He was able to make out a room about fifty feet away that had light coming out of it. It was not sunlight but man-made halogen light. This was where the motor noise was coming from. Carefully he hugged the walkway wall and came closer. When he was about twenty feet away he heard two men's voices coming from inside the room where the light came from. He could not make out their words. He came closer and stopped about ten feet away from the door opening, hugging the wall.

- - - - - - - - - - - - - - - -

"I told him to meet me here. I don't know what's keeping him." Major Britin was speaking with the doctor inside the infirmary. He was irritated at being kept waiting by Jess.

- - - - - - - - - - - - - - - -

Jesse could make out voices, but the noise from the motor muffled what they were saying. He strained to hear. Suddenly he heard someone approaching from down the walkway that he had just come. He panicked. He turned his head and looked for a place to hide. Without any real choice he ran back to the first room he came to and scurried in.

The room was like all the others along this section of the fort. There was a small window opening in the center of the outside wall, through which sunlight came. Unlike the other rooms along the walkway, this room had scuba equipment stored in it. This was the gear that was going to be used for the President's dive. He recognized his tanks and wet suit. This was the storage room.

The person coming along the walkway was getting close. Jesse, picking up one of the single air tanks that was stacked next to the gear, threw himself against the inner wall next to the door opening and waited. The footsteps came right up to the doorway and stopped.

- - - - - - - - - - - - - - -

Jess was late. He was now wearing fatigues. He had been busy at the other end of the fort and misjudged the time it would take to get here for his meeting with the Major in the infirmary. As he came up to the storage room, he decided to have a quick look to make sure that everything was in place. He was already late and wasn't concerned about a couple more minutes. He turned and entered the storage room.

- - - - - - - - - - - - - - -

Jesse readied himself for whoever was about to

enter the storage room. He raised his arms and brought the tank above his head. It was not very heavy, but would certainly do the job he needed it for. He could not take the chance of being discovered.

Jess walked through the door and into the storage room. Without warning he felt the sudden hard impact of something on the back of his head. His knees buckled and he fell to the floor and lost consciousness.

Jesse brought the air tank down hard upon the back of the head of the soldier. There was a clank as it impacted. The stunned soldier hesitated, wobbled, and then fell to the floor. Jesse stood overtop him clutching the air tank, ready to strike again, but the soldier did not move.

Satisfied that he had done the job well, Jesse put down the tank and bent down to grab the arms of the soldier to drag him out of the doorway. He pulled the soldier into the corner behind the scuba gear and turned him over.

"What the?" Jesse was startled. He was looking at himself. His mouth dropped in disbelief. This was the clone. He had hit the clone.

Whether planned or not, Jesse had now determined the path he was to follow. He would have to switch with him right away. The clone would be missed and that would alert Major Britin.

As Jesse changed clothes with the clone, he was amazed by the accuracy of the carbon copy before him. Everything was duplicated exactly. He could have been looking in a mirror. He felt strange being here with the clone and stranger yet at having hurt him. Though he had never seen the clone before, Jesse had a strange affinity for him, like he was a brother. But he knew that this was not his kin.

While these thoughts swirled through his mind, Jesse quickly changed clothes. The clone, now dressed in his clothes, lay motionless on the floor. Jesse was standing in the military fatigues above and looking down at himself. For a moment he wasn't sure if he was really who he was or someone else. Maybe he was a clone as well and didn't know it. These thoughts sent a chill of fear up his spine. He shook himself back to reality and tried to recover from the experience. Though Monika had described the clone to him, Jesse had always believed that he would be able to discern a difference, but he couldn't.

- - - - - - - - - - - - - - -

"I'm going to find him." Major Britin had waited long enough. He was angry. He stormed out of the infirmary and started up the walkway. When he came to the storage room he slowed and looked in.

"Captain Ehrlich!" he shouted recognizing the soldier within.

- - - - - - - - - - - - - - -

Jesse was startled by the loud bellowing voice at

the entrance to the storage room. He turned and visually identified the Major. He had been discovered. He was thrown instantly into his new role.

"Sir," he answered reflexively, his navy experience taking over.

"What are you doing here? Why are you keeping me waiting? Do you think I have nothing better to do than wait around for you all day?" He wasn't pleased.

"Sir. I...was attacked..." Jesse pointed to Jess lying upon the ground.

Major Britin followed his pointing hand.

"What the?" he stuttered as he saw the body.

"Sir. I don't understand." Jesse played the part he believed would work. He would pretend that he had been attacked by this unknown man and, after he had disabled him, was shocked to discover he was his look-a-like.

The Major rushed over to the body, not understanding what had really happened, or who the look-a-like really was. Was it the real Jesse or the clone? He put his fingers against the body's neck. He felt for a pulse, but couldn't find one. There would be no interrogating the intruder. He ripped the press pass away from the look-a-like's shirt and held it in his hand as he considered what he should do. He never considered that the soldier standing behind him was anything other than the clone. He quickly made up a story so as not to alarm the clone any more than necessary. He needed him to remain calm and unsuspecting until the President was delivered.

"He's dead. Someone was trying to get to the President," Britin began.

"I don't understand Sir." Jesse didn't realize he had hit the clone so hard, but he wasn't affected by the outcome. He was glad he had survived. The clone was the enemy.

"You hit him hard Captain. We won't be able to ask him. Someone has gone to a lot of trouble and plastic surgery to look like you."

"Why Sir?" Jesse continued playing the part. His shock at discovering the clone helping him transfer successfully into this new role. Major Britin believed him.

"I don't know. Someone wants to get to the President through you and now you've stopped him." Britin stood up and faced Jesse. He examined the clone closely, looking for any sign of deception. "Good work Captain."

"Thank you Sir. It's a little unsettling." Jesse didn't flinch.

"That's why we have so much security."

"But how did he get this far?"

"He used this." Britin waved the press pass in front of him. "He must have snuck over here with the media."

"What do we do with him? Should I alert the Secret Service, Sir?"

"No." Britin was firm. "We don't…We don't know who's involved. We'll keep this between us. I'll look into it and alert the other men. Understood Captain?"

"Yes Sir." Jesse stood to attention. From the tone of the Major's voice he knew he was being given an order and responded accordingly.

"Now give me a hand. We'll move him out of here."

"Yes Sir." Jesse came over and grabbed Jess's legs. The Major grabbed his arms.

"We'll take him to the infirmary." Britin could hide the body in one of the canisters.

The two men struggled with the dead weight of the body. They left the storage room and went the short distance down the walkway to the infirmary.

"Dr. Pearl. We have a patient for you." Britin announced their entry.

"What's wrong?' The doctor rushed over to them as they held the body. When he saw the dead body he became speechless. He didn't understand what was going on. He looked to the Major for some sort of explanation.

"He attacked the Captain, but he won't be bothering him again." Britin made a face so the doctor would understand not to say anything. "Help us put him in one of the empty canisters."

"Over here." The doctor directed them across the room and opened one of the empty canisters. "Put him in here."

The Major and the Captain lifted the body into the canister. The doctor closed and locked it.

"Captain. Why don't you go and get a coffee and relax. I'll see you later at the orientation." Britin used a gentle paternal tone to dismiss him. He wanted to have some time alone with the doctor.

"Yes, Sir. Thank you Sir." Jesse saluted. He was relieved that he had gotten away with the switch and happier still to be able to get out of the infirmary.

"Don't say a word about this. That's an order," the Major's tone became firm.

"Yes, Sir." Jesse saluted, turned and left the infirmary. Major Britin remained silent and stared questioningly after him.

"What's going on?" the doctor demanded of the Major.

"I don't know."

"Who is that?' The doctor meant the body in the canister.

"I hoped you could tell me. How many clones were made?"

"Just two of him, and one was disposed of, off Ft. Lauderdale."

"Are you sure."

"As far I know that's all. Unless Mr. Fence had more made."

"Why would he do that?"

"I don't see a reason."

"Then who is it?"

"Maybe it's the original."

"No. He's in the brig at the base. I would have been notified if there was a problem."

"Then I don't know. What are we going to do?"

"Nothing. We go as planned. Will the Dive Master be okay?"

"I think so. It shouldn't affect his programming."

"Good. We've come a long way. A lot of planning has gone into this operation. We've only got a few more hours and this will be over. Let's not screw it up."

- - - - - - - - - - - - - - -

Jesse hurried down the walkway toward the command center. He could not go back to Monika. It was too dangerous. If they knew she was here he would be exposed. She would have to fare without him. He hoped he would have an opportunity to let her know he was all right. Maybe at the orientation. He knew all about the itinerary and the layout of the command center from the briefings he had attended weeks ago. He hoped he hadn't missed or forgotten anything important. He hoped that the Major would not suspect him before Monika could safely expose the plot and he could protect the President. So far he had been lucky, but there was still a lot to come.

- - - - - - - - - - - - - - -

Monika thanked the soldiers and went into the ladies room. She wondered what had happened to Jesse. She wasn't sure what she should do. The ladies room consisted of a walled-in room with one large window space open to the ocean. Three portable outhouses were lined up against one wall and two eighteen-inch by two-foot mirrors were placed on the wall opposite them. There was no door in the brick doorway that led out to the promenade, just a partition that had been temporally angled in front of the doorway to prevent any unwanted wandering eyes.

Monika waited a few minutes to give the soldiers time to leave and then exited the washroom. Once back in the promenade, she decided to go outside to the docks and wait for Jesse there.

The crowd of media was still intense around the entrance to the fort. Monika made her way amongst them and went down the grassy path to the docks. She stopped about twenty feet in front of the REPUBLICAN QUEEN. Carolynn was standing on shore near the stern chatting with some colleagues. She recognized Monika and excusing herself from the small group, came over. Monika seemed upset to her.

"Hi. Did you get everything unloaded?"

"Oh yes." Monika was distracted and kept looking up to the fort for any sign of Jesse.

"Where's your cameraman? Jesse wasn't it?" Carolynn sensed that something was wrong.

"Oh. He's in the fort setting up." She tried to appear calm but knew that her old roommate was suspicious of her behavior.

"What's up? Really. You can't fool me. I've known you too long." Carolynn came closer and lowered her voice.

Monika knew that Carolynn would not give up until she had unearthed the truth, or something that she wanted to believe was the truth. She had gone into the right profession. Monika had to make something up. She remained silent.

"Come on. What's going on? You can tell me. Is it about Jesse?" Carolynn continued to probe. She had sensed something between these two on the trip from Key West. Jesse was more than Monika's cameraman.

Monika saw her opportunity and nodded. A tear fell from her eye onto her left cheek.

"Oh you poor thing. Come with me. Let's go on board and have something to drink. You can tell me all about it." Carolynn comforted her friend. She was pleased that she had not been wrong about Jesse and Monika. She put her arm around Monika and escorted her to the gangplank at the stern. They got on board the ship and headed for the upper deck. Monika stole one last glimpse of the fort entrance before going up the stairs but there was still no sign of Jesse. She hoped he was safe. She wasn't sure what she would do if she couldn't find him before the President's arrival.

"Don't you worry about him. I'll take care of you. Men are all the same." Carolynn saw Monika searching the fort entrance and assumed she was looking for Jesse, her lover. She hurried Monika up the stairs. She wanted to hear all the sordid details.

Chapter 15

At 1900 hours Agent Gorman and Major Britin stepped onto the platform that had been temporarily built on the northwest parade section of the fort. Major Britin sat down on a chair that was placed behind a microphone stand next to a large map of the fort. The map was mounted on a stand facing the crowd. Most of the media were in attendance and standing together in a large crowd on the ground in front of the platform. They were conversing loudly with each other, but when Agent Gorman came up to the mike and started speaking, they settled down and listened. It was bright and warm out. The sun had not yet set.

"Good evening ladies and gentlemen. My name

is Agent Aaron Gorman. Behind me is Major
Britin. Welcome to Ft. Jefferson. I'm here to ori-
entate you regarding tomorrow's schedule. If you
don't mind, save your questions until the end…"

- - - - - - - - - - - - - - - -

Jesse was standing off to the east side of the
platform. The Major wanted him close by in case
there were questions about the dive that he could
not answer. Jesse had spent the afternoon at the
command center. He had not been able to make
contact with Monika. He hoped that she would be
at the orientation. He hoped he could somehow
make contact with her. He was scanning the
crowd while Agent Gorman started his orientation. He was not listening to the words coming
over the speakers. He was focused on the crowd
and his search for Monika.

- - - - - - - - - - - - - - - -

"The President will arrive at 1100 hours, land
here in the south of the parade grounds. You will
be able to set up your cameras here and here."
Agent Gorman referred to the large map.

- - - - - - - - - - - - - - - -

Monika and Carolynn stood at the back of the
crowd. Monika was wearing one of Carolynn's
power suits, and her hair was pinned up. It fit her
nicely. She looked very sophisticated.
She and Carolynn had had a drink and then
Carolynn had suggested that Monika borrow
some of her clothes and not go back to her boat

for hers until after the orientation. Monika had agreed. They had had fun trying on the clothes and comparing likes and dislikes. Being about the same size, Monika and Carolynn had always shared clothes during their years as roommates at Stanford. It had helped stretch their meager student's wardrobe.

- - - - - - - - - - - - - - -

"He'll go inside to the south section and the unveiling ceremony will take place here. After the ceremony he will change into scuba gear and go to the moat for the dive. There isn't a lot of room out there so we ask that you stay in your assigned location for the photo op."

- - - - - - - - - - - - - - -

Not seeing Monika, Jesse slowly backed away from the platform and began to walk the perimeter of the crowd. Major Britin did not notice him leave. He walked around the crowd searching for any sign of Monika. When he got near the back he caught a glimpse of her standing with Carolynn. She looked so different in her new outfit that Jesse had to check twice to be certain it was her.

- - - - - - - - - - - - - - -

"Major Britin. Could you talk a bit about the dive?" Gorman turned to ask the Major to come up to the stand.

The Major got up and came to the mike.

- - - - - - - - - - - - - - -

Monika also scanned the crowd for any sign of

Jesse. As she scanned the east side of the crowd her eyes caught a glimpse of a blonde haired soldier in fatigues making his way around the back of the crowd. Monika recognized him, but didn't know if it was Jesse or Jess. She stared at him.

- - - - - - - - - - - - - -

"The President is going to dive in the moat to see the artifacts on the bottom. There are a number of cannons and other relics that have been found there."

- - - - - - - - - - - - - -

Jesse's eyes met Monika's. He could see her confusion. He mouthed the words: "It's me. OKAY."

Monika saw the soldier mouth some words to her and then bring his index finger up to his lips to indicate: 'Be quiet.' This had to be Jesse. Her heart raced. He was safe and must have made the switch. Carolynn was watching the platform and had not witnessed Monika and Jesse's communication.

- - - - - - - - - - - - - -

"It should be an interesting dive and I know the President is looking forward to it."

- - - - - - - - - - - - - -

Jesse began to walk toward Monika. He wanted to have a chance to speak with her in the relative anonymity of the crowd.

- - - - - - - - - - - - - -

I'd like you to meet Captain Ehrlich. He will be

in charge of the dive." The Major turned to his left to introduce the Captain, but he was gone.

- - - - - - - - - - - - - - - -

Just as Jesse was making his way over to Monika, he heard his name called out. He stopped dead in his tracks and turned away from her to face the platform. He realized that he would not be able to talk to Monika now that the attention of the crowd was upon him.

- - - - - - - - - - - - - - - -

"Captain Ehrlich? Are you out there?" The Major covered his embarrassment and addressed the crowd.

"Here Sir." Jesse called out from the far side at the back.

All eyes were turned in his direction. Carolynn and Monika also looked after him, but they could only see his back and a bit of a profile. He was not recognizable to them. He had turned to face the platform.

"Oh there you are. Captain Ehrlich is a veteran Dive Master and will be in charge in the moat." The Major turned to Agent Gorman. Agent Gorman came up to the mike and continued the orientation.

"Thank you Major, and Captain. After the…"

- - - - - - - - - - - - - - - -

Jesse did not look back as he made his way to the front of the crowd. He did not want to risk being identified by Carolynn or associated with

Monika. He quickly became lost in the crowd which was again focused on Agent Gorman. He hoped that Monika had understood his message and realized that it was him and not the clone.

- - - - - - - - - - - - - - - -

"I didn't see him." Carolynn was curious. "What was he like." She meant Captain Ehrlich.

"I didn't see him either. He was over there in the crowd with his back to us," Monika lied. She had clearly seen him and was privately trying to understand the mouthed communication.

As Agent Gorman continued the orientation, Monika ran the scene over in her head. Jesse had definitely infiltrated Britin's camp and switched with the clone. It was now up to her to expose the plot and all the players in it. She knew that she had to try and talk to Jesse before the President arrived.

- - - - - - - - - - - - - - - -

Dan and James were almost at Garden Key. The fort loomed on the horizon. The sun was just beginning to set. The cloudless sky was full of red, yellow and violet hues, which were magnificently reflected on the water. They were tired after the long ocean journey. They had been given a small 'banana boat' to use and the ride had been rough. Banana boat was the nick-name given to the long narrow powerful boats found along the Florida coastline, that were purchased more for their incredible speed and social statement than

their comfort. They were loud and brightly painted. They were the 'Hot Rods' of the ocean.

When they came within a hundred yards of the
fort, one of the Secret Service boats motored up to
them and flagged them to stop. Dan, who was driving, slowed the engines. The two boats came
along side of each other.

"Agent Anstey? Detective Swan?" There were
two men in the boat casually dressed in the same
style of Secret Service pants and top, wearing
dark sunglasses and ball-caps. The one of them
who was holding the two boats together asked
their identity.

"Yes," James answered for both of them.

"Can we see your identification?" he requested.

"Yeah." James pulled his out of his pocket and
presented it to the agent. Dan passed his along
through James.

"That's fine Sir." The agent returned both pieces
of ID to James. "You can moor up alongside at the
dock. The command center is in the south section.
Agent Gorman is expecting you."

"Thanks." James took back the documentation
and the agent let go of the boats.

Dan powered up and they pulled away from the
Secret Service boat, heading for the dock.

- - - - - - - - - - - - - - - -

The orientation did not last long. Monika and
Carolynn had returned to the REPUBLICAN
QUEEN immediately after it ended. There was a

party being thrown onboard and Carolynn had invited Monika to attend. She liked being reunited with her roommate.

Monika was trying to plan her next steps but there was nothing she could do until later tonight. She had to try and sneak into the command center. It had to be done tonight before the President arrived, before the security in the fort tightened up. She decided to try to enjoy herself for a couple of hours. When the party was over, she would slip away.

- - - - - - - - - - - - - - - -

Dan and James waited in the command center for Agent Gorman. It was about ten o'clock. Agent Gorman had been radioed regarding their arrival while he was attending a party on the REPUBLICAN QUEEN, He was just now making his way to the command center. He wondered why these two men were here on the island and how they had gotten clearance so easily.

"Gentleman. Sorry to keep you." Agent Gorman came into the command center.

"James Anstey." James offered his hand and shook with Gorman.

"Dan Swan." Dan did likewise.

"What brings you to Ft. Jefferson on the eve of the Presidential visit?" Gorman sat down behind the table as he asked. He got right down to business. He didn't like being disturbed by what he considered liabilities before the President's arrival. They would only bring more work and bad luck, and he didn't welcome either.

"Have you seen this woman?" James pulled out a photograph of Monika and presented it to him.

Agent Gorman took the photo, but did not recognize the woman.

"No. I don't." He handed it back to James. "Should I?"

"We have reason to believe that she is here," Dan lied.

"So? Is she some sort of threat?" Gorman became interested.

"We don't know," James continued, not wanting Dan to make up the story. "She disappeared two days ago in Key Largo."

"And what has that to do with me or the President's visit?"

"We suspect foul play," Dan added.

"But what has that got to do with the President's visit here at Jefferson?" Agent Gorman didn't see any connection to warrant these two men being here.

"We're not sure, but we think it's connected." James realized how absurd they both appeared, but wasn't going to reveal Monika's message.

"You're not sure? On the eve of the President's visit and you're not sure? It seems a bit of a long shot to come out here on a missing persons. I've got the whole island secure. Nothing's going to happen to the President. How's it connected?"

"We think she's stumbled onto something that involves his visit here tomorrow," James added. "But we don't know what. That's why we'd like to find her. We think she's here somewhere on the island."

"You're welcome to look around, but I think you're barking up the wrong tree. It would be hard to get here. There's too much security. She's probably just taken off. Maybe she's hiding out from a boyfriend. That's how these cases usually end up," Gorman joked. He didn't like having his time wasted and he now viewed this as a waste of his time.

Dan looked at James for guidance and a response. He didn't like Gorman's attitude.

James was stone-faced. He took an instant dislike to Gorman and his insinuation. He was about to reveal that Monika was his girlfriend and that she hadn't run off, but decided not to respond or laugh at the bad joke. Dan followed suit.

Gorman felt suddenly discomfited, by the two men's unresponsiveness.

"As I said, gentlemen. Feel free to look around. Let me know if you find anything. I don't expect that you will be sleeping tonight so I won't assign you quarters. There's a lower level to the fort and the media is at the northwest of the island. It's very straightforward." Gorman stood up. "If you'll excuse me, I've got other matters to supervise. Good luck." He walked away from the table.

"Nice fellow, isn't he?" Dan said in a sarcastic tone.

"Yeah," James agreed, though he wondered if Gorman's attitude wasn't justified. Was Monika really here on the island and had she really stumbled upon something involving the President's visit?

"Let's start looking around. She's got to be here somewhere." Dan, sensing James' state of mind, encouraged. "We can start in the lower level."

- - - - - - - - - - - - - -

Monika left the party around 11:30 PM. It was still going strong and no one noticed her leaving. She made her way to the fort and was now walking inside along the southeastern section of the vaulted promenade. It was dark inside, being only lit by the moonlight shinning through the window openings. She felt a shiver of cold. Most of the media were partying on their boats and the sound of their revelry echoed into the fort. The only other sound she could hear was that of the rolling waves against the breakwater. Most of the Secret Service and Major Britin's men were in their camp preparing for the next day. From midnight on they would all be on high alert and scattered throughout the fort and island. They were enjoying their last minutes of down time. This was the calm before the storm of the Presidential visit. The only guard who remained on duty had been at the main entrance, and he had not bothered her other than to ask to see her press pass.

Monika carefully made her way along through the looming silence in the vaulted promenade, which reminded her of a crypt. She came up to the stairwell that Jesse had hidden on. She stopped and considered whether or not she should go down and investigate. She decided she had no other option. She had to try and find Jesse.

The stairwell was dark. Monika ran her hand along the cool rough surface of the brick wall as she gradually descended the stairs. When she got to the bottom, she found herself in the same walkway that Jesse had been in earlier. There was just enough moonlight shining in the corridor to allow her to continue her search. Her pulse was rapid and her mouth was dry. All of her senses were heightened in her fear of being discovered.

- - - - - - - - - - - - - - -

Jesse was in the camp with Major Britin and the other men of the corp. After the orientation the Major had brought both Dr. Pearl and him along to the encampment to have dinner. He wanted to keep both men in sight until they were in position and ready for the President. He liked to spend time with his men before a mission. It made him feel more connected to them. He felt that everything was secure and was unaware of the arrival of Dan or James on the island. He had left a skeleton watch in the fort with his counterpart, Agent Gorman, in charge. At midnight the operation was to begin. Until then they all had time to relax together. The Major was determined to make this mission successful. Jesse would not be able to go anywhere unescorted before the President's arrival. He was too important a part of the operation and Major Britin, after finding the body, wasn't taking any more chances.

- - - - - - - - - - - - - -

Dan and James had searched most of the lower level of the fort for any sign of Monika. It had taken longer than they expected. It had been difficult to search those parts of the fort that were not illuminated by generated light. Though they had used the small flashlights they had brought with them, the darkness of the interior of the fort in some places was too heavy for their small beacons of portable light to fully penetrate. Now coming along the walkway by the infirmary, they were relieved to be back in the illumination of the halogen lights.

The lower level, from the infirmary up to the command center, had been well lit. They had found nothing unusual so far. They had encountered a couple of guards but, because of their clearances from Agent Gorman, they were left alone and allowed to roam. Having completed their search of the southern section of the fort, they stopped for a moment in the light of the infirmary.

"Where to now?" Dan asked.

"Let's take a look around the north part of the fort," a discouraged James replied. "Maybe we could get something to eat at the encampment?" He had hoped to find some clue that would lead him to Monika, but he hadn't. He was beginning to believe that she was not here, and the he had been mistaken in his assumptions about her whereabouts. He wondered where she really was and why she had left her cryptic message.

- - - - - - - - - - - - - - - -

Monika stared down the walkway. She thought she could hear the drone of a motor of some kind running in the distance. She began a slow walk southward toward the sound. She soon saw the glow of a light in the walkway about a hundred feet away, but couldn't identify its source from this distance. She was not far from the infirmary. She became more cautious in her approach, but was still drawn like an insect in the night to the light's magnetic beam. Her curiosity was roused. She wanted to know where the light was coming from.

She continued down the walkway, hugging the wall for another fifty or sixty feet and was soon within thirty feet of the light source. She stopped and, hidden within a masonry doorframe, reconnoitered the area ahead as best she could.

Two men were standing talking in the walkway about thirty feet away. The light was emanating from an open door beside them. She could not make out their words. The sound of the motor was drowning them out. She carefully crept along the walkway to better hear them. The light was so bright upon them that she felt certain their eyes would not be able to adjust to the darkness that cloaked her. She came within twenty feet of them and stopped, hiding herself again within the darkness of another doorframe.

"Did you see something?" James thought he had seen something in the shadows farther up the walkway.

"No." Dan was facing the other direction.

"Over there. Something by the doorframe. There. Don't turn 'round," James spoke in a low voice. He sensed that someone or thing was watching them.

"Okay. What do you see?"

James nonchalantly peered and tried to see along the walkway. There was a cable from the generator in the infirmary running along the floor of the walkway to the doorframe where he believed someone was hiding.

Monika crouched in the doorframe. The two men were still talking but she was unable to hear what they were saying. On the floor below her a cable ran along the floor and into the room beside her. The room was lit only by the moonlight. She took a quick glance. There was equipment of some kind stored inside.

"Let's slowly go up the walkway. Act casual.

Keep an eye on that door." James began to go up the walkway. Dan pulled out his gun and was close behind him.

Monika saw them coming. She didn't think that they had seen her, but they would if she didn't find a better place to conceal herself. They were coming her way and there wasn't much choice or time to plan. If she turned and ran down the walkway, they would instantly see and chase after her, or worse. If they had guns, they could easily shoot her while she tried to run down the walkway. She would be a sitting duck. She was not willing to take that chance. The storage room beside her was the only place she felt she could safely sneak into and not be found.

Keeping her eyes on the two men who were by now only fifteen feet away, she side-stepped into the storage room.

The room was full of boxes, scuba tanks and other equipment. Monika searched the room as best she could in the half-light. The urgency of hiding before the men reached the room was upon her. She hoped they would pass by, then she could find her way out and back to the safety of the REPUBLICAN QUEEN.

She crossed the room and wedged herself behind some of the crates that were placed against the fort wall adjacent to the doorframe and waited. She could not see out from her hiding place. Her heart was racing and her adrenaline surged.

She tried to calm herself and listen for the two men, but her own body sounds pulsating in her ears prevented her from hearing well. She took in deep breaths and tried to slow her heart rate.

"There. In that room. I saw something." James, who had been using all his ability to see in the dark, saw a movement through the door. Moreover, he had a strange sensation that something was there. He couldn't explain it. He actually felt the presence of someone. "I'll go in first. You stay in the doorway."

Dan nodded.

James came to the storage room first and slowly entered the room. It was dark inside. Only a small ray of moonlight was shining through the tiny window in the outer wall. He scanned the room for anything obvious but could not see anything moving. He spotted a halogen light on a stand in the far corner opposite all the equipment and boxes that were stacked against the wall to his right. He indicated to Dan behind him that he was going to go to the light and turn it on. He crossed the room and fumbled with his right hand upon the stand to locate the light switch.

Monika was terrified. The men had entered the room. They must have seen her. Panic set in. She pushed herself lower into hiding and closed her eyes in fear. If she was quiet, she believed they might not find her. She began to shake uncontrollably. The flight / fear reaction within her was hard to control.

James found the switch and twisted it. The halogen light atop the stand came to light and the dark room was suddenly bathed in its blue-white glow. Both he and Dan squinted while their eyes adjusted to the sudden burst of illumination.

The room was definitely being used as a storage room. It wasn't very big. There were scuba tanks and gear stacked against the wall, and small crates of other equipment placed next to them around the room. James began a careful visual search.

Monika crouched down as far as she could behind the wood crate as the lights came on. These men were very thorough. She was extremely nervous and afraid, and felt like a cornered animal. She cowered and tried to minimize any noise that her pounding heart was making. She felt certain that they would hear her, its pounding was so loud in her ears.

Dan stood motionless in the doorway pointing his gun into the room. James' attention was drawn to the equipment and wooden crates opposite him. They both stood silently observing the room.

Monika's left leg cramped and she pushed against the crate, causing it to move. There was no sound to its movement. She brought her left hand down to the cramp and tried to work it out without causing any more motion against the crate.

James saw the crate move. He had the intruder

trapped. He looked over to Dan and indicated his discovery to him. Dan smiled and prepared himself in case the intruder tried to escape through the door.

"Come out," James' voice was firm. "I know you're there. Behind the crate. Come out. NOW,"

Monika heard the voice. She had been discovered. She didn't react immediately as he considered what she should do.

"Come out or I'll shoot." James didn't have a gun but he would try and scare whoever it was out.

The man's voice sounded familiar, but in her panic, Monika could not place it. She straightened her legs. The pain from the cramp was not gone. She raised up her arms and slowly began to stand up to face her captors.

James watched as a pair of slender surrendering arms were pushed out from behind the crate. They belonged to either a young boy or—a woman! James was startled.

"Don't shoot. I'm coming out," Monika said before revealing herself. She looked out from behind the crate to the man who had threatened her.

"Monika?" James instantly recognized his fiancée. "Monika?" A lump grew in his throat. He was not able to speak.

"James!?" Monika was flabbergasted. Her chest grew heavy and she began to weep. "Oh James."

James ran across to her and they embraced. They hugged and kissed. She felt his powerful body against hers. His arms holding her firmly. His rough bearded skin against her cheek. His soft hair. His scent. She was overjoyed at his presence. How she had missed him. She squeezed tightly against him, instinctively molding her body against his. She felt a surge of excitement within her. She was safe and he was here.

"What are you doing here?" Monika asked as she reined in her emotions. James kissed her lips and then her cheeks, while holding her face in his hands. Monika was smiling ecstatically.

Dan watched the reunion from the door. He holstered his gun. He was grinning and could see how much in love James and Monika were. It made him feel good to see two people so devoted to each other and deeply in romantic love. He wished he had a relationship like that.

"I played a hunch. I got your call and came right away. I thought I'd lost you," his voice softened as he spoke the last sentence. He gazed into her beautiful big sparkling blue eyes. Her blond hair framed her face.

"Oh, I love you sweetie." They hugged again.

"Ah hem." Dan cleared his throat.

"Oh, Dan. This is Monika Queller. My fiancée." James turned and, still holding Monika, introduced her.

"I thought as much. Hi." He smiled.

"Hi." Monika returned the smile but Dan could see that she was more enthralled at being in James' arms and reunited, than meeting him.

"We should leave before someone comes." Dan sobered them back to the reality of their circumstances. "You can talk more after we get out of here."

Dan was right. Both James and Monika put the questions they had for each other on hold.

"Okay Dan. You go first. I'll get the light. Monika. Stay between us."

James went back to the stand and turned off the light. The room instantly returned to darkness. It took a few moments for their eyes to adapt to the weak glow of the moonlight that now lit the room and walkway.

Dan went out into the walkway. Monika and James joined him. Just as they were beginning to go, they heard the sound of people coming from ahead.

Dan took out his gun. "Quick. Back into the room," he alerted them.

They all ran back into the room and found places to hide.

Two soldiers were coming down the walkway. The loud sound of their footsteps rang out over the sound of the generator in the infirmary. They came closer and then stopped in front of the storage room.

Dan was pushed tightly against the brick wall

concealed to the left of the door and James was similarly positioned opposite. Monika had hidden behind the same wooden crate as before. Dan indicated to James to get ready.

"Thanks Corporal. I'll be okay now. I'll see you on your next round." Jesse spoke loudly so the other soldier, his escort, could hear him.

Major Britin had insisted that Jesse be escorted to his post. He didn't want anything to happen to him. The soldier was to deposit him safely and then go on guard duty around the command center. The whole fort would now become an impregnable fortress. No one would be allowed into the command area without special clearances. The safety of the President demanded this type of security.

"You're welcome, Sir." The soldier saluted and continued on down the walkway.

Jesse watched after the Corporal. Once he was gone, he turned and went into the storage room.

"Now where's the light?" he muttered to himself as he entered the room.

Hearing Jesse's steps and his proximity, Dan and James tightened their bodies in preparation. Dan held his gun close to his chest pointing out into the doorway.

Jesse took two steps into the room and was pounced upon without warning. Dan, in one swift action, put a strangle hold around Jesse's throat and shoved the gun hard into his back. He pulled the soldier deeper into the room.

"Don't make a noise, or you're dead," Dan threatened.

Jesse was taken by surprise. He did not struggle. He understood the danger he was in. He brought his hands up to Dan's arm to lessen the pull on his throat and felt the gun pressing into his lower back all in the same instant.

"James get the light." The guard in the walkway outside would expect to see the light go on after Jesse entered the storage room.

James scurried over to the light and switched it on. Monika came out from hiding and viewed the scene before her. Jesse was being held by Dan, whose arm was strangling him, and a gun was poked in his back.

"Monika? You're all right," Jesse managed to note despite being choked.

"Let him go." Monika was alarmed and she commanded Jesse's release without thinking twice.

Dan looked to James questioning Monika's request.

"I know him. He's one of us. Let him go. You're suffocating him." Dan still kept his grip. Monika changed her tone. "We need him."

James, understanding Monika's tone, nodded his approval to Dan. Dan gradually lessened his grip and backed away a couple of steps, but kept his gun aimed at Jesse.

"Whew. Thanks," Jesse was sarcastic to Dan. He didn't appreciate being manhandled.

"I thought…I didn't know what to think when you didn't come back. Did you find him?" Monika came over and addressed herself very personally to Jesse. Both Dan and James observed the two. They seemed to know each other well. Monika's voice was gentle. James felt a tinge of jealousy.

"Yeah." Jesse was comforting his neck. "He's dead."

"Dead?" Monika was alarmed.

"It was an accident. There was a fight. I hit him…They don't suspect a thing." Jesse explained.

"Hey. Do you mind filling us in?" James interrupted.

"Oh sorry. This is Jesse Ehrlich. The real one. He's in charge of the President's dive tomorrow, or today."

"The real one?" Dan questioned.

"They're cloning people. They're going to switch the President. That's what this is all about." She opened out her arms to indicate the scuba gear.

"Cloning? That's not possible. They'd never get away with it." James found it hard to believe.

"Yes they would and they have. They've found a way to upload a person's entire memory."

"But how?" Dan was curious.

"Believe her. I've seen it for myself. It's real." Jesse confirmed.

"They cloned Jesse to get close to the President. I met him, the clone, and couldn't tell the difference. They are going to switch the President with a clone and upload him with his memories so no one will know. Then they will be able to control the country. They needed Jesse to grab the President in the moat and make the switch. It's all happening within the next twelve hours."

"Who's involved?" James was beginning to believe Monika. It was an incredible tale. One that he thought would only be true in science fiction but obviously it wasn't.

"Major Britin. I'm not sure if his men know all about his plan, but they're involved. There's a doctor as well," Jesse started to answer James' question.

"They kept us prisoner in an abandoned base in Key West," Monika continued.

"I know that base. It hasn't been used for years. It's kept boarded up," Dan spoke up.

"Well it's being used now," Jesse corrected.

"We managed to get away and find our way here to stop them." She directed her next sentence to James, "You didn't call me back."

"I tried. You left the phone off the hook at my parents'."

"What about your cell?"

"The battery went dead and I couldn't recharge

it. I wasn't expecting to come here so suddenly."

"Okay you two. There'll be time for that later. What are we going to do now?" Dan intervened.

"We have to do something, but I don't know who we can trust. I don't know who else is involved with the Major. Maybe the Secret Service is involved. Who knows?" Monika refocused her thoughts away from James and onto the issue at hand.

"Yeah. This could involve some of them. They need to have insider help to pull this off." Though Jesse was correct in his supposition, he had no real proof of his hypothesis.

They all fell silent for a few moments while they each tried to come up with something.

"Well, we can't all stay here. That guard will be back soon." Dan was correct. There was not much time to waste. They had to move quickly.

"Jesse." Monika had an idea.

"Yeah."

"Can you hide two of us here until the President's arrival?"

"Yeah. There's a couple of empty crates. You could use them. I don't think anyone will look in them. I'm the only one allowed in here."

"Good. Then I think I have a plan that will work. We will have to do it all ourselves, but I think we can pull it off. What time is it?"

"12:15," Dan checked his watch and called out.

"Then we'd better hurry. He's right. The guard

will be back soon and the security around here will be impossible to get by. We can't leave here together. This is what we're going to do."

- - - - - - - - - - - - - - -

Major Britin and Dr. Pearl entered the main entrance of the fort. The two men did not speak. They were in a hurry. They wanted to check out the infirmary and Captain Ehrlich to make certain everything was going according to plan. It was 12:30 AM. In a matter of hours it would be all over.

As they walked along the promenade the rhythmic sound of the Major's heavy military boots reverberated along the shadow-drenched corridor. It was reminiscent of a scene from an old Nazi Germany war movie.

Chapter 16

At 10:59 AM Marine One descended from far up in the sky to the south parade grounds of the fort. Along with the seal of the President, the large white UNITED STATES logo was painted on its dark gray side and could be easily read. A perimeter around the landing area was set up. Major Britin's men, along with half a dozen Secret Service agents, were guarding the site. Some of the media had cameras and crews located on the grounds just beyond the security ribbon. Other cameras and crews were stationed within the promenade level of the fort looking out. Everyone was positioned for his or her best possible vantage.

The large two-toned Presidential helicopter

came lower and hovered above the site. A great
swirl of dust was whipped up by the downdraft of
its blades. The noise of the engine ricocheted
against the inner fort walls. Gradually its wheels
touched firmly upon the ground, then the engines
were cut and the downdraft slowed to a stop.

Major Britin rushed out to meet the helicopter.
The main loading door opened and two Secret
Service men, dressed in dark suits and wearing
dark aviator sunglasses, jumped from the helicopter's opening and placed a small set of steps
from the door to the ground. They then took up
positions on either side of the opening, staring out
onto the parade ground, and waited.

Several minutes passed. A striking clean shaven
man with graying neatly kept hair, appeared in the
helicopter door. He was dressed in a dark gray
perfectly fitted suit, with a formal gray tie. He
stood in the opening and waited a couple of
moments while he viewed the landing site. The
whirl of dust caused by the landing settled. It was
the President. A wave of excitement rushed
through the fort. It was as if a movie star had
arrived and his loyal fans were eagerly awaiting
his entrance. All attention was focused on the
man.

The President stepped down to the parade
ground and waved. Major Britin saluted the
Commander-In-Chief and welcomed him to the
fort. There was clapping as the two men made

their way to the command center of the fort.

"Too bad your friend is missing this." Agent Gorman was standing in the command center along with James watching the arrival. They were waiting in a cordoned off area where the unveiling ceremony was to take place, away from the crowd of media standing beyond them. The media was packed-in like sardines onto the promenade of the command center.

"Yes. He's very ill. It must have been the seafood we had yesterday," James mumbled in a distant tone.

"Well it will all be over soon and then you can get him down to the infirmary. Maybe they can help him out."

"Yeah. I'll try that."

"No sign of the girl?" Gorman never turned to face James while he spoke. Both men were watching the progress of the President's arrival.

"No. Nothing."

Agent Gorman smirked.

"Well. Here we go," James changed the subject as the President entered the fort.

Clapping followed the President as he made his way through the throng of media. Major Britin was beside him and several of his men helped to barricade them from the crowd in the command center. James and Gorman stepped forward as the President and Major Britin came up to the small area where they stood. The area was taped-off with a special ribbon bearing the Presidential seal. They were to be the President's protection. Under other circumstances, when the perceived threat was greater, there would have been far more security in the room, but the space was too tiny and did not permit it. The President stood about five feet to the side of them.

"Ladies and Gentlemen. The President of the United States." Major Britin stepped up and introduced the President to the waiting crowd. The President moved forward.

- - - - - - - - - - - - - - -

Down below, in the infirmary, Dr. Pearl was preparing his equipment. He was with a diver who was dressed in a black wet suit that completely covered him from head to toe, making him unrecognizable. The diver was there to help transport the clone through the drain and out to the moat and then return with the President.

The room was quiet. Two soldiers were stationed in the walkway outside, one in front of the infirmary and one in front of the storage room. They were under strict orders not to allow anyone to enter or leave the area until after the visit was over.

Dr. Pearl opened the canister containing the sedated clone of the President and injected a stimulant into his arm. The stimulant would rouse the clone enough to allow him to accompany the diver. The clone wore scuba gear that matched the

President's. Major Britin and the doctor had dressed him a few hours earlier. He was ready for the dive.

As the clone awoke, Dr. Pearl and the diver helped him out of the canister. He was zombie-like and cooperative. The three men crossed the infirmary to a large drain that was covered with a metal lid. While the diver supported the clone, the doctor lifted the lid to reveal an old drain that was originally used as an escape route from the fort out to the moat. It was circular and contained an old iron ladder that was attached with heavy black bolts to the masonry.

"Come on. Hurry. Get him inside and out to the opening in the moat," the doctor directed the diver.

The diver complied without saying a word. He got into the drain and the doctor helped the clone in after him.

"Once you switch the President get back here fast. There won't be much time," the doctor reminded the diver.

The clone and diver disappeared into the drain. The doctor put the lid back in place and returned to his equipment. Everything was ready. All he needed now was several minutes with the real President to complete the downloading process.

- - - - - - - - - - - - -

The President's speech had been short. He wanted to get to the dive. Once the plaque was unveiled, Major Britin led him out of the command center and down to the fort's lower level. Thanks to the generators, the stairs and walkway were brightly lit. It had only taken a few minutes for the two men to arrive at the storage room. As they walked by, the guards stood rigidly to attention and saluted. The President acknowledged them with a nod of his head.

"Captain Jesse Ehrlich," Major Britin came into the room with the President. "The President."

"Sir. Good to see you again." Jesse saluted and smiled. Jesse was already dressed in his gear.

"Captain Ehrlich." The President's tone was formal. "It's been a long time. Key Largo wasn't it?" The President remembered him from his pre-Presidential years.

"Yes Sir. You haven't changed at all Sir." Jesse smiled. He was amazed how personable the President was. He had expected him to have changed once he had taken office, but he hadn't.

"Thank you Jesse. Just the weight of office," he jokingly tapped his stomach. Though in good shape, he was heavier than the last time they had met.

"I've got your gear all laid out."

"Major. Give us a few minutes alone," the President asked the Major to leave.

"But Sir. I…" The Major did not want to leave the President unattended.

"It's okay. I'll be okay. I need a little privacy."

"Yes Sir." The Major had no choice. He understood. The President didn't want to have an audience while he changed from his business suit to his wet suit. He turned and left the room. Jesse and the President were alone.

- - - - - - - - - - - - - - -

Using his flashlight, the diver and the clone made it down the ladder to the bottom of the drain about five feet below the infirmary. The ladder ended in a pool of water. The diver stepped off the last step and splashed into the water. The clone followed. They could not touch bottom. The wall and water absorbed their flashlight making it hard to see. With difficulty, they swam through the water and found the underwater continuation that led to the moat. The drain ran horizontally out from the infirmary's vertical entry to the moat and was a little larger in this section. Side by side, the diver swam with the zombie-like clone through the drain. It was a haunting place. Algae covered the walls. It was dark and claustrophobic. Fortunately it was a short dive. Within twenty feet, the darkness of the drain suddenly changed and the two arrived at the opening to the moat. The water was murky, but the brightness from the sun above found its way to them.

The diver pulled the clone with him out into the moat. It was difficult to see very far ahead or above. They settled and remained stationed at the bottom of the moat next to the drain opening and waited.

- - - - - - - - - - - - - - -

Wearing their gear, Jesse and the President exited the storage room. They both had on their wet suits, tanks and masks. Major Britin accompanied them along the walkway to the temporary stairs and the opening to the moat. All three men climbed down the newly constructed wood stairs that led out from the walkway and the promenade above to a small dock-like floating wood platform. As they stepped onto the platform the crowd of reporters clapped their welcome. The President waved to them all. Jesse led the President farther out into the moat along the platform.

"Mr. President. I'll get in first. Then you follow. Remember to stay close. It's kinda murky down there." Jesse gave the thumbs-up and the President returned the same physical communication.

"Sir," Jesse addressed the Major for permission to begin the dive.

"Go ahead Captain." The Major gave his approval to commence, aware of the fact that they were all under the close scrutiny of the cameras. He realized that it was now all up to the Captain to make the mission successful. He hoped his programming was working.

Jesse got down on the platform and slid into the moat. Once in, he indicated for the President to follow. The President, helped by the Major, got down on the platform and lowered himself into the water. Both he and Jesse floated next to the platform.

Along the breakwater and from the promenade of the fort, the media and security looked on. There was a small boat with an outboard motor attached floating on the moat about forty feet away. Two Secret Service men dressed in scuba gear were seated in the boat.

Jesse gave the thumbs-up again to the President. Both men adjusted their masks, put in their mouthpieces and submerged below the surface.

The water was a dirty-brown color. The two men began to swim. Jesse was in the lead. The President followed. The brightness of the sun permeated about five feet down and then the water became murkier. The two swam into the murkiness and faded from the sight of those on the breakwater above. They swam straight down. There was a lot of debris on the bottom and they could only see a few feet around themselves. It was eerie. They swam in the direction of the drain opening.

- - - - - - - - - - - - - - -

The Major, along with the crowd, watched as the President dove into the moat. They observed as he and Jesse went deeper and then disappeared into the murky water. All that could be seen of the divers was the trail of exhaled air bubbles from their regulators that floated and popped along the moat's surface in the direction they were swimming. Major Britin checked his wristwatch. It would not be long now.

- - - - - - - - - - - - - - -

Major Britin's men were guarding Marine One. After the President had landed and gone into the fort, the captain and his crew disembarked to stretch their legs for a few minutes. They did not venture away from the helicopter, but remained to one side of it on the parade grounds. Without being noticed, one of Major Britin's men managed to sneak onto the helicopter and make his way into the cockpit. Several minutes passed and he re-emerged, having successfully disabled the craft. It would take the pilot a long time to discover the problem after he unsuccessfully tried to start the helicopter, but it would only take a few minutes to repair it.

- - - - - - - - - - - - - - -

Jesse spotted the two other divers at the bottom of the moat and stopped. One, the clone, remained stationary against the moat bottom while the other diver lunged at Jesse and grabbed the President. There was a struggle. The diver produced a syringe and injected it into the President's side. The President reacted in pain and pulled away in the water, but it was too late. He rapidly succumbed to the injected drug and went limp. It had all happened quickly. The diver grabbed hold of the President. Jesse swam over and helped him drag the limp form through the water to the drain. He waited as the other diver took the President deeper into the drain. He watched as the two disappeared and then swam over to the clone, who was beginning to float upward and held him securely in place.

- - - - - - - - - - - - - - -

Dr. Pearl was anxiously awaiting the return of the diver with the President. He was pacing the floor in the infirmary around the lid to the drain. He hoped the Dive Master's programming had kicked in. He looked at his wristwatch. They should be back soon. He bent down and removed the lid and waited for them.

- - - - - - - - - - - - - - -

The Diver made his way back along the drain with the semi-conscious President. It was a difficult swim but he soon found his way to the drain under the infirmary.

Breaking through the water, he pushed the President up onto the iron ladder. The lid to the infirmary was open and light from the room above illuminated the drain by reflecting on the rippling water below. Dr. Pearl stretched down to assist in bringing the President up while the diver pushed from below. He grabbed the President's right arm and pulled him out of the drain and onto the infirmary floor. The diver quickly climbed up and got out, carefully placing the lid back onto the drain. They were in a hurry. The doctor immediately assisted the diver in first removing the scuba tanks and fins from the President and then his own. They left the gear in a pile on the floor. It would be easier to move around without all that weight.

With the aid of the diver, Dr. Pearl lifted the President into the chair that was set-up for the downloading. The President flopped down. The diver backed away. Dr. Pearl was nervous and his hands shook. With difficulty he straightened the President up and removed his mask. He then started to remove the rubber headpiece of the wet suit. Gradually the head piece came off and revealed...

"Who's this?" Dr. Pearl was shocked. The man in the wet suit was not the President. He turned to get an explanation from the diver. "What's going on?"

The diver was standing in front of him. He was holding a small caliber handgun and had it pointed at him.

"Don't move." It was a woman's voice. The diver removed her mask and pulled off her rubberized headpiece.

"What the?" The doctor was stunned. "It's you."

"Yes doctor. It's me. Surprised?" Monika was standing before him, her hair and female features now more apparent.

"But how?" Dr. Pearl didn't understand.

"It's a long story." She waved the gun threatening-ly. "Just get back."

The semi-conscious man in the chair was detective Swan. Dr. Pearl backed away and Monika crossed over to check on Dan. Dan mumbled incoherently. Monika was concerned.

"It's just a mild sedative. It won't last long. He'll be okay." Dr. Pearl was nervous.

"You'd better be right." Monika's tone was harsh. She disliked the doctor and wanted to get even for the way he had treated her at the base.

- - - - - - - - - - - - - - - -

Major Britin checked his watch. It was about time. He wondered if Jesse had successfully completed his part of the mission. He watched at the surface of the moat near the fort wall. The amount of air bubbles was increasing.

"Yes," he thought to himself. "That's the sign." He could safely put the next part of the plan into operation.

"Something's wrong," he called out to the divers in the boat on the moat and pointed to the air bubbles rising to the surface.

His sudden outburst echoed along the fort wall and the breakwater. Everyone's attention was drawn to the Major and then the bubbles in the water. There was a surge of activity as the media honed its cameras onto the surface of the moat.

The two divers immediately understood the rea-son for the call and dove into the water. A tense silence prevailed as they disappeared below the surface and swam deeper into the moat.

- - - - - - - - - - - - - - -

Jesse had waited long enough. He grabbed onto the still groggy clone and swam away from the fort wall back to the surface. Suddenly out of the murkiness of the water he saw two divers swimming toward him. The divers came over and hurriedly grabbed onto both he and the President and started for the surface.

As the group broke the surface of the moat a cry of shock came from the crowd. Jesse tore the President's mask off his face and held him on the surface with the help of the other divers. The President was unconscious.

"I don't know what's happened," Jesse said as he ripped his mouthpiece and mask off. "He suddenly stopped swimming and panicked."

The men, cradling the President's masked face above water, swam for the platform. James and Agent Gorman, having heard the Major's alarm, had rushed from the promenade to join the Major and were waiting by the water as the divers came to the platform. They all bent down and helped to lift the unconscious President out of the water and laid him flat upon the platform. The Major knelt down to check the President's condition, according to plan.

"He's breathing. Let's get him to the infirmary." He took command.

A horrifying panic set into the crowd. There was pandemonium as the scene of the President lying motionless on the platform sank in.

"Here. Give me a hand. Quickly!" Major Britin ordered as he removed the President's air tanks.

James, Gorman and another soldier came to assist the Major. They lifted the President up and carried his limp heavy body off the platform to the stairs. They hurried up the stairs into the fort's lower level heading for the infirmary. The crowd of media swelled forth upon them.

"Keep them back," the Major ordered to the Secret Service and his own men who had also rushed over to protect the President. "Get the President's helicopter running. We'll be there soon," he said to Agent Gorman. "We're okay here."

"John, Philip, Mark," Gorman understood and called out to his men who were following to the walkway. James, the Major and the other soldier were capable of getting the President into the infirmary. It was his and his men's job to get the President off the island to whatever care was required.

"Come with me." Gorman stopped with his men, allowing the President to be taken away. There was enough security with Major Britin's men to control things in the infirmary. He brought up his left wrist as he stood and spoke into a microphone.

"The President is down. Everyone in the fort converge on the parade grounds." His voice was radioed to all of his men in and around the fort. He lowered his arm.

The President was carried away to the lower level of the fort. Agent Gorman went into action. All his training had taught him not to react as a normal citizen in a time of emergency. He had been taught not to allow panic or fear to frighten him. He and his men had been taught to react rapidly and effectively without wasting the tiniest moment in any reaction that caused them to turn or back away from the emergency.

He and his men climbed up the stairs and made their way through the crowd. Questions were being yelled out to him from the media which was being held back and out of the way by Major Britin's men.

"Sir. Can you tell us what's happened?"

"Agent Gorman. Is the President alive?"

"Where is the President?"

"Where is the President now?"

"Where are you going?"

"Will you be taking the President to Key West?"

"When can we see the President?"

Agent Gorman ignored them and pushed through onto the promenade. He was not stopping. He crossed through the promenade and out onto the parade grounds where he and his men ran to Marine One.

"Get it going," Gorman yelled as he approached the Marines standing in front of the craft.

The Marines weren't sure exactly what was going on, but knew that something had happened to the President. The security around the helicopter increased as most of Agent Gorman's and some of Major Britin's men, who had been elsewhere in the fort, reacted to the news of the President. They followed their training and converged on the command center to concentrate their protection.

A human barricade was formed to hold back the crowd. A general panic had set in. It was important to secure the area and maintain a clear path for the President.

"You guys give them a hand," Agent Gorman ordered his men to help the others on the parade ground as he came to the helicopter.

The pilot, co-pilot and crew were now onboard. The pilot was trying to start the engine but it would not ignite. Agent Gorman jumped into the helicopter and climbed up to the cockpit.

"Captain. Get this bird going."

"I'm sorry, Sir. It won't start."

"Well find the problem and fix it! I want this bird up and running right away," Gorman ordered.

"Yes, Sir!" The Captain knew the reason for the urgency and accepted his orders without further comment. He didn't want to let the President down. He started going through all the checks and procedures to discover the cause of the malfunction.

"Radio for back-up. Just in case."

"Yes Sir." The Captain complied as his co-pilot continued the check. "This is…" he began his call to the closest base which was Boca Chica.

Agent Gorman turned away and went back to the helicopter's open door to wait for the President to be brought to the parade grounds from the infirmary for transportation. The whine of the helicopter's engines trying to start drowned out the shouts from the media. They were complaining about being kept away by his men. Gorman prayed that the President was all right. He wondered how this could have happened. He would have a lot of difficult questions to answer after this was all over.

- - - - - - - - - - - - - -

Dr. Pearl was standing in the center of the infirmary when the loud commotion of the President being brought down the walkway reached him. Monika was standing next to Dan who was still seated in the chair, slowly becoming more lucid.

"Soldier. Allow no one by," Major Britin ordered the guard in the walkway near the infirmary door. The other soldier from the storage room had joined the guard and together they had hurried over to be of assistance to the President. Major Britin, James and the soldier, who had carried the President from the moat, entered the room.

Monika looked up and pointed her gun at the men entering the infirmary. They were all caught off-guard.

"What's going on here?" Major Britin was stunned to see Monika and even more alarmed to see Dan and not the President, dressed in the President's wet suit, semi-conscious in the chair.

James let go his hold on the clone, backed away and pulled out a gun, leaving the soldier, who didn't really understand what was going on, with the Major, holding the President. The guards at the door, having seen this act, turned into the room and aimed their weapons. They were confused. They went into an automatic reaction to protect their President and the Major.

"Don't move. Any of you," Monika shouted out to them all. James aimed his gun at the guards. Major Britin, the doctor, the soldier and the President were caught in the middle of all this firepower.

"Corporal," Major Britin used his strongest tone of command to one of the guards at the doorway. "Protect the President. Shoot them."

"That's not the President," Monika yelled.

The guards were baffled.

"She's right. It's not. It's a clone. He's trying to switch them," James added. "Don't make a mistake. It's true."

"Tell them doctor!" Monika threatened Dr.

Pearl.

"I don't know what you're talking about." Dr. Pearl looked to the Major for guidance. He was more afraid of what the Major would do to him than Monika.

"If that's true, where's the real President?" one of the guards demanded. He was in turmoil as to who he should believe.

"In the storage room," James responded.

"Don't be a fool Corporal. It's a trick," Britin complained.

"If you don't believe me, check. I'll come with you and she'll stay here."

The Corporal considered. The idea was so far-fetched that he and his cohort didn't know what to do, but they didn't want to make a mistake that might cause harm to the President or the Major.

"Corporal. I'm giving you an order. Protect the President. Shoot them."

There was an awkward pause as the Corporal tried to understand what he should do and who he should listen to.

"I'm sorry Major, but I think we should check-out the storage room."

There had been an underlying tinge of panic in the Major's voice. This tone made the Corporal doubt the Major's sincerity. It was an instinctual reaction. He had never heard the Major quite so edgy before and, as the President was involved, he had a higher duty to be certain of his actions.

The Major let go his grip of the President, forcing the soldier to support the full weight.

"Okay Corporal. Go and check it out." Britin realized he could not force the Corporal to act against his will. He put on his best poker face pretending to call James' bluff. "We'll be okay here for a couple of minutes. You go with him, but Sergeant," he addressed the other guard, "You stay here."

The compromise made, James looked over to Monika, who still had her gun aimed at the Major in the center of the room, to confirm his departure from the infirmary. Monika nodded her consent. Carefully he left the room and went into the walkway after the Corporal, keeping his gun drawn to prevent him from making foolish moves. They both went down the walkway to the storage room.

"Sergeant. Come in here and help," Major Britin was about to play another hand. He had to get away before they returned. Maybe the real President was in hiding in the storage room. Only he and the doctor knew that was a possibility and that the unconscious man on the floor in the center of the room was not the President but really a clone. His thoughts were now on escape and no longer on completing the mission.

Monika remained firm. She was obviously nervous. She had no experience in this type of situation. These men thought the man before them was the President and that he needed their assistance.

She needed to gain their trust for a few moments longer until James returned. And when he returned with the real President, it would be a matter of who was more credible, the Major and his clone, or James and the real President?

"Slowly, and put your gun down." Monika set her rules.

"Do as she says, Sergeant."

The Sergeant lowered his weapon and came into the room.

"Lift him onto the table. Over there."

The men lifted the clone and carried him over to the operating table. Monika was nervous and felt uncomfortable with all the movement. She was losing control and she didn't like it. James was taking an eternity to return.

"Doctor. See what you can do," Britin took advantage of the opportunity. The doctor read Britin's thoughts and came over.

As the doctor began to cross the room, Monika followed and the Major made a lunge at her. The gun discharged and a bullet hit the doctor. Everyone else in the room took cover. The doctor fell as a single bloodstain oozed from his chest. He had a look of outright amazement upon his face as he fell to the floor.

Major Britin was undeterred by the event and grabbed the gun from Monika. She stood frozen in shock. She had never killed anyone before and felt like throwing up. Britin grabbed hold of her.

"Sergeant. Protect the President."

"Yes Sir." The Sergeant bounced back into action.

"I'm going for help. I'm taking her. Cover us until we're out of the walkway."

"Sir." The Sergeant crossed the room and took up his post at the door. He watched down the walkway for the others.

- - - - - - - - - - - - - - -

James and the Corporal entered the storage room and were about to open one of the larger crates when the sound of the shot echoed out along the walkway. Both men stopped, ran to the doorway and peeked into the walkway.

"Stop right there. The girl's shot the doctor. Bobby keep him there. The Major's going for help," the Sergeant poked his gun into the walkway and yelled.

The Corporal took advantage of the confusion, cocked his weapon and stuck it into James' back.

"I wouldn't move if I were you."

"It's a trick. Don't believe him."

"We'll just wait and see," he said to James, then shouted back, "Jimmy. It's okay. He ain't going nowhere."

"Sir. It's clear," the Sergeant informed the Major, who was behind him with Monika as hostage.

"Come on. Shut up and act normal or you're dead." The Major pushed her ahead with the gun.

They both made their way into the walkway.

"James?" Monika screamed out as she was led out into and down the walkway.

"Shut up, or you won't see him again," Britin threatened one final time.

"Monika?" James watched as she and Britin rushed down the walkway.

"You're making a mistake," he aimed his comment at the Corporal.

"You're the one who's making the mistake. Now shut up."

- - - - - - - - - - - - - - -

"Here's the problem." The pilot discovered the sabotage. Two wires had been severed from the ignition panel. "Someone's sabotaged us."

"Can you fix it?" the co-pilot asked.

"Yes. It's not serious. Just a minute." The pilot pulled out his pocketknife, bared the wires and then wound them together. "Let's try that."

The whine of the cranking motor began and this time the engine started. The helicopter was operational.

Agent Gorman was pleased that the pilot had fixed the helicopter. He was waiting onboard at the door facing onto the parade grounds. The spin of the helicopter blades was picking up speed and the down draft was beginning to swirl up the sandy soil on the parade grounds. All these things had occurred at the same instant that Monika's gun had fired inside the lower level of the fort, muffling the shot from being heard outside.

- - - - - - - - - - - - - - -

"They've shot the doctor. Go and help!" As the Major and Monika went down the walkway, Britin announced this news to the soldiers that were stationed at the stairs to the promenade.

The soldiers had heard the shot and wondered what had happened. They did not think to question their commander. They took off down the walkway to the infirmary. Britin pushed Monika up the stairs. He would not have any problem with his men on the level above.

- - - - - - - - - - - - - - -

Agent Gorman saw the Major exiting the fort with Monika. He wondered why he was coming this way without the President. The rest of the helicopter's flight crew was back on the parade ground awaiting the President's arrival, in case he needed assistance getting onboard. The swirl of sand forced everyone in the vicinity to protect their eyes. Neither Agent Gorman nor the crew were able to spend long examining the Major's and Monika's arrival. In moments they were at the helicopter.

"Major. How's the President?" Agent Gorman helped them both onboard and shouted above the din. The crew on the ground behind him was waiting for the Major's answer.

"He's fine." Britin presented and pointed his gun at them. "But you won't be if you don't do what I say."

Agent Gorman was stupefied. The crew remained still.

"Now get off. Hurry!"

- - - - - - - - - - - - - - -

"I'm telling you Corporal. It's a trick. I'm with the CIA. I can prove it. The real President is in here. Let me show you." James needed to prove to the Corporal that he was telling the truth. He wanted to stop the Major and rescue Monika.

"You can keep the gun on me. Just let me show you," he pleaded.

"Show me." The Corporal was willing to call what he believed was James' bluff.

James carefully pulled out his wallet from his shirt pocket and gave it to the Corporal. The Corporal examined it. It contained authentic look- ing ID.

"How do I know it's real?" The Corporal was still unconvinced.

"Trust me. Just for a few minutes. If I'm lying you can shoot me."

The Corporal weighed it over. "Okay, but no tricks." He handed the wallet back to him and James returned it to his pocket.

With the Corporal behind, James crossed the storage room and began to open a large crate that was lying on the ground.

"Mr. President. It's okay. It's James Anstey." James called out loudly. He tugged at the wood and the lid opened. To the Corporal's amazement a duplicate President stared back at them.

"Mr. Anstey. I thought you'd forgotten about me." The President was slightly worn but in good spirits.

"No Mr. President, but we have a situation." He indicated the Corporal who, though dumfounded, was still pointing his weapon at James.

"Corporal. Don't just stand there. Help me out of here," the President commanded, using a tone that he knew the Corporal would react to.

"Yes, Sir." The Corporal, accepting that this might be the President, wasn't taking any chances. He put down his weapon and, with James, helped the President out.

"Corporal. Believe me when I tell you that this is the real President. The other's not. Trust me."

"Yes Sir." The Corporal really didn't know what to believe, but he was beginning to seriously doubt the Major.

"I've got to go after them. Okay?" he questioned the Corporal.

"You heard him Corporal. Now stand down," the President added the strength and authority of his office to his voice.

"Yes, Sir." The Corporal reluctantly accepted. It was very convincing. He was not willing to make a mistake and offend his Commander-In-Chief.

"Mr. President. You'll be safe here."

"Go ahead Mr. Anstey. Give 'em hell."

- - - - - - - - - - - - -

Jesse had followed up the platform after the President was carried away. He had begun to climb the stairs but was stopped by Britin's men and told to wait on the platform. He had waited patiently, hoping that everything was going according to Monika's plan.

- - - - - - - - - - - - - -

"Jimmy. We're coming out. Everything's okay," the Corporal shouted into the walkway.

"But the Major said to stay put."

"I know, but everything's okay."

James and the Corporal went into the walkway.

"What about him?" the Sergeant, seeing James, was uneasy about letting James go free. The two soldiers from the stairs at the end of the walkway were standing behind him.

"Don't worry. I'll accept responsibility. Go on Mr. Anstey."

"Thanks." James sped along the walkway after Britin.

As James came to the stairs at the end of the walkway that led out to the moat and up to the promenade, Jesse spotted him.

"James. What's going on?" he called out.

James stopped.

"Britin's escaped with Monika. We've got to stop them."

Jesse hurried into the walkway. The soldiers had gone and there was no one left to stop him.

305

"I'm coming with you."

"Come on. Hurry."

The two men sped up the stairs to the promenade.

Agent Gorman moved away and the Major slammed the helicopter door closed. There was no crew other than the pilot and co-pilot aboard Marine One.

From inside the helicopter, the Major had a clear view of the cockpit.

"Get this thing outa here," he waved his gun and ordered.

The pilot had no choice.

"They're taking off!" James stopped on the parade ground about fifty feet away from the helicopter. Jesse didn't know what to say. There was nothing they could do.

The helicopter revved up and lifted higher into the air. When it was eighty feet from the ground it began to fly southeast away from the fort.

"Where will they go?" James stared up at the helicopter.

"If they keep that heading? Cuba." Jesse suggested.

"Cuba? He's got Monika. We've got to stop him."

"How?"

Agent Gorman and the remaining crew, having

seen James and Jesse come out from the fort, rushed over to them.

"Where's the President?" Gorman demanded.

"He's safe in the fort. In the storage room. I'll explain later."

Gorman raised his arm and spoke into his mike, directing his men to the storage room.

"What about them?" James continued.

"There'll be another helicopter here anytime. It's been called in."

- - - - - - - - - - - - - - -

Major Britin was pleased that he had managed to escape. He watched as Ft. Jefferson fell into the distance. He felt relieved that he was free, and imagined himself on the sunny island of Cuba.

"Sir?" The pilot interrupted his musing. "Where are we going?"

Major Britin was annoyed by the interruption.

"Cuba."

"Sir?"

"Cuba. Now shut up and get us there."

The pilot gave a look to his co-pilot and reluctantly did as he was told.

"I hope you like the beach, Ms. Queller. 'Cause you're going to be spending a lot of time there." He began to laugh.

Monika stared helplessly out of the window at the vast ocean below and Garden Key in the distance. She felt at a loss.

- - - - - - - - - - - - - - -

"There it is." Agent Gorman pointed out the arriving military helicopter. "I can only let you come along."

James understood and turned to face Jesse.

"Go ahead. I'll stay." Jesse patted James on his shoulder as he spoke. "Don't let them get away."

"I won't."

The helicopter was an old UH-1 gun ship, a HUEY, and was painted dark green. Its sliding side doors were open. It began to descend to the parade ground. Agent Gorman, James and the others cleared out of its way. Sand blew up and around creating a miniature sandstorm.

The HUEY was louder and bigger than the President's helicopter. A large gun was mounted on its right side next to the panel door opening. A Marine, dressed in green fatigues with a bulky helmet and sun visor that was pulled down over his face was standing in the opening and tethered by a thick strap to the inside. There was a microphone protruding from the helmet in front of his mouth.

As the helicopter touched down, it did not stop its engine. James and Agent Gorman bent down and ran out to the helicopter and the Marine.

"Good afternoon Sir. We were in the area and got your call. We're the closest help. How's the President?" he politely and calmly shouted above the noise of the rotor. James, having arrived ahead of Agent Gorman, pulled out his ID and quickly flashed it in front of the Marine. The Marine was in his early twenties.

"The President's safe inside the fort, but we have to stop Marine One. There's a hostage on board."

"Climb on board."

James and Agent Gorman were helped in. No sooner had Agent Gorman stepped off the ground into the HUEY, than it started to lift off the ground and fly southward.

The Marine attached tethers to both of the men. James firmly held onto a handle inside the large payload section of the helicopter. It was windy and noisy and dangerous, but he did not have time to be concerned for the carnival-like ride experience.

"They went southeast," James leaned over and shouted.

The Marine nodded and spoke into his microphone. The helicopter began to fly in the direction of the fleeing helicopter.

Ft. Jefferson fell behind them quickly. The HUEY was a fast craft. The three men sat down on the floor of the compartment and silently waited.

- - - - - - - - - - - - - - -

"I don't think either of us will be going to Cuba." Monika grinned as she spotted the other helicopter coming into view behind them.

Major Britin leaned over and looked out the

window. He saw the large gun ship closing in on them. He had not anticipated that another craft would have been able to respond so quickly. It must have already been in the area on some kind of maneuvers. He kicked himself for not being prepared for this eventuality. They would not be able to outrun their pursuers. There was only one thing he could do. He made his way over to the cockpit.

"Go down," he threatened the pilot with his gun.

The pilot begrudgingly responded by pushing the stick forward. He had to do as he was told. The helicopter began to descend.

"You," Britin motioned to the co-pilot. "Come here."

The co-pilot looked to the pilot who nodded his approval. The co-pilot unbuckled himself and got out of his seat. Major Britin kept his gun on him and they both went back into the passenger section. The Major shuffled the co-pilot with Monika next to the door to the outside.

"Open it," he ordered the co-pilot to open the passenger side door.

- - - - - - - - - - - - - - - -

After a couple of minutes, the Marine received a message from the pilot.

"They're straight ahead Sir," he informed both of them. "They're going down." The Marine was keeping both men informed of the information he received from the pilot.

James stood up and, holding tightly onto the handle at the side door opening, leaned out and looked ahead. The wind blew strongly against his face. The President's helicopter was not far ahead of them and it was descending to the ocean.

- - - - - - - - - - - - - - -

The co-pilot opened the door. The wind and noise penetrated the compartment. The helicopter had descended to about fifty feet above the surface.

"Grab her."

The co-pilot, understanding what Britin intended, did not respond. Without warning, Major Britin fired. The bullet surprised the co-pilot, hitting him in his stomach and pushing him backward. He fell with a cry out of the opening. Monika attempted to save him but was too late.

"What are you doing?" Monika protested.

"You're next." Britin ignored her.

"Don't. Please. Don't do this," Monika pleaded.

Britin let go his grip and came closer to the opening. Monika stood by the side of the opening holding onto a small railing.

"Either you jump or I shoot." Britin was adamant.

Monika looked out.

- - - - - - - - - - - - - - -

James gasped as he saw someone fall out from the President's helicopter and splash into the water. The man was dressed in a flight suit.

"Man overboard!" was all he could think to shout. It was clear from the way the person hit the water that he had not survived.

The Marine informed the pilot and the HUEY suddenly slowed and rapidly descended.

- - - - - - - - - - - - - - -

The ocean was about fifty feet below. It was a dangerous leap, but Monika realized it was her only choice.

"What about a life jacket?"

"It's more interesting this way," Britin smiled. "Now get out."

Monika took in a deep breath and resolved herself to the leap. The wind was blowing her hair wildly. She squinted her eyes. She had been a member of the Stanford dive team, but the highest dive she had ever made did not compare to this. She knew she would have to jump straight out and hope she hit the water feet first. She was terrified, but she had to jump. It was hers and Britin's only hope. Bolstering all her courage, she let go of the handrail and stepped out.

Monika screamed as she fell. There was a feeling of lightness within her as she sped feet first through the air. She did not like the feeling. It made her feel sick to her stomach. Seconds later she felt the impact of the water. Her wet suit protected her from the impact. She stole a breath before she was submerged below the ocean's surface.

- - - - - - - - - - - - - - -

"Down! Go down!" James screamed to the Marine. He watched as Monika had fallen and splashed into the water. He was horrified at the prospect of losing her. She disappeared for a few seconds below the water and then bobbed back to the surface. She was panicking in the water. He could tell she was trying her best to get her breath, remain afloat and survive the ordeal, but she needed help.

The HUEY was soon overtop and hovering about forty feet above her. James could see the fear in Monika's face. Without thinking, he undid the strap that held him safely in the helicopter and jumped out to attempt her rescue. Both Agent Gorman and the Marine were caught off-guard by his sudden irresponsible action and leaned out to watch as he impacted the water below near Monika. They were surprised that he made the jump in one piece. He bobbed up from below the surface and swam over towards Monika. She swam for him. It did not take long for them to be reunited. Once together, they embraced and kissed, and tried to stay afloat together. The down draft from the HUEY was rippling the water around them. They were safe. James looked up and smiled, giving the thumbs-up signal.

"Sir," the Marine inquired of Agent Gorman as they both watched. "What about the President's helicopter?"

"Don't worry about it, soldier. They're more important." Agent Gorman smiled. "Let's get them out of the water. We've had enough action for one day. The politicians can sort the rest out."

- - - - - - - - - - - - - - -

Major Britin grinned as the helicopter behind gave up the chase. He was safe. His plan had worked. He had hoped they would stop to save the girl. It had given him the time he needed to get away. In a matter of minutes he would be in Cuba, far from the reach of American authorities.

Epilogue

Towering above the New York skyline, the Microtech building commanded a powerful view of the city. In a large office decorated in the most expensive taste, William Fence sat at a desk with his back turned to the room and gazed through the large ceiling-to-floor window.

A well-groomed man in dark business attire was standing on the other side of a large mahogany desk. A small television was turned on and could be heard in the background. A news reporter was covering the story of the aftermath of the recent incident involving the President at Ft. Jefferson. He was standing on the steps outside the Federal Court in Washington DC reporting on the indictment of Dr. Pearl and Colonel Brookland and their plot against the President.

"They've interrogated the clones: Hemings and the Colonel, but Britin is still in Cuba. They won't be able to connect you. The clones won't remember you—or our involvement. Their programming will hold." The man was referring to those aspects of the reporter's story.

Fence turned around to face his assistant. He had heard enough of the news report. He was not happy at the outcome of recent events.

"And what about the originals?" Fence no longer was paying attention to the television and the sound of the reporter's voice faded into the background of his mind's awareness.

"They're still in our care. No one knows." The assistant had an air of confidence about him.

"Good. And the President?"

"The White House is busy reporting this as a case of plastic surgery and a terrorist attempt to assassinate the President. They don't want to reveal the truth to public. They're busy spinning it to their advantage."

"But they know?"

"They know about the clone, but they don't know where it came from."

"We'll have to put the next phase into operation right away." Fence was pensive. "And this time no mistakes."

"We already have, sir. We still need the President's download. We think we'll be able to get it at his next annual check-up at Bethesda. Everything is being put into motion as we speak. We'll be ready in six months. The girl was an unpredictable aberration and it won't happen again."

Fence turned his chair and stared out over the skyline. He imagined Bethesda Hospital where the President would soon have his annual check-up. He imagined the doctors and nurses and staff who would look after the President during his short stay and how they would all be cloned and programmed to do his bidding. He chuckled at the prospects. Sooner or later he would have what he wanted. There would be no escaping him.

"It better not." Fence responded as he continued to stare out over the New York City skyline. His voice was hard and menacing.

$\underline{\text{S Y N O P S E S}}$

MYSTERY NOVELS

OBSESSION

A Novel By Bestselling Author:

Terence Munsey

SYNOPSIS

After her family dies, a young woman, Monika Queller, and her friend, James Anstey, are stalked then chased to San Francisco, where they stumble upon a secret.

Monika Queller's parents mysteriously die in a car accident. Their bodies are never recovered. Her father was a research scientist at Stanford

University. Unable to bear the pain of her loss, Monika decides to start her life over, away from the reminders of her tragedy. She moves to Los Angeles where she takes a job as an adult education teacher.

Once settled in Los Angeles, strange things begin to happen to Monika. She is stalked, receives prank calls, her car is vandalized, finally her home is broken into and vandalized. She is at a loss to understand and turns to a colleague, James Anstey, for help. Unknown to Monika, James is an undercover CIA agent who has been placed to protect and keep an eye on her. Monika's father was working on top secret experiments and his death is suspicious.

Monika discovers a note from her father, which was hidden in his old briefcase. The note directs her to go back to San Francisco and collect something from a post office box at the university, but she does not know what it is she will find there.

As Monika and James start out on their journey, they find themselves being followed by an unknown pursuer or pursuers. Soon they are being chased. They decide that they must try to get to the university before whoever is after them can catch them—it is their only hope of solving the mystery. Along the trip, Monika and James become romantically involved.

Once at the university they retrieve an envelope from the post office box and are waylaid by their pursuers. James is taken captive, but Monika manages to escape with the aid of Bill Meyers, an FBI agent who also has been following both of them.

Monika discovers that her parents are not dead. A ransom demand is made by James' captors for his safe return—the envelope for James. Working with the San Francisco FBI office chief, Mical Grai, and Bill Meyers, Monika agrees to the exchange. Grai is one of the bad guys. He is after Monika's father's secret research, though Monika and Meyers are not yet aware of this fact.

Further complicating the plot and without Grai knowing, James is rescued by another undercover operative, William, and an exchange meeting is arranged at Fisherman's Wharf. William's undercover operation suspects Grai and is hoping to set him up—he wants to expose and arrest Grai.

At the exchange Grai panics once he realizes that he has been set up. He takes Monika and tries to escape capture. Grai manages to get to his car and with Monika, attempts a get-away. Unfortunately the attempt is foiled when Monika struggles with Grai inside the car; a struggle that causes the car to crash and sink into the harbor.

Monika awakens in the hospital. She was rescued from the harbor, but does not remember anything after crashing into the dark cold water other than being trapped with Grai in his car and then passing out.

Now awake and recovered the mystery is revealed to her. Grai is dead. Monika's parents are alive and by her hospital bed. The story ends as Monika is reunited with James, with whom she has fallen in love.

EMERALD CITY

A NOVEL BY BESTSELLING AUTHOR:

TERENCE MUNSEY

SYNOPSIS

A gripping thriller involving subterfuge, and international intrigue, set in the most sophisticated city of the world.

The story opens with a brutal murder of a couri- er, Ted Ambrose, in the first class lounge at Toronto International Airport. It is a professional hit. The bag that Ted is transporting is handcuffed to his wrist and the killer is forced to hack-off Ted's wrist to get the bag.

Two weeks later, Monika Queller, our heroine, is on her way to Toronto to participate in the Harborfront Writer's Festival. While at the festival she encounters the son of the murdered courier, Andrew Ambrose, who convinces her to help him to prove the involvement of ABM COMPUTERS in his father's murder.

ABM has developed a new chip technology that allows them to access all the data on any of their new computers that contain the chip. By offering free internet access and voice mail capabilities on their computers, ABM encourages owners of their computers to leave their machines permanently connected to the phone lines and switched on. Through their new product registration lists, ABM is able to gain all the information needed in order to gain access to the data on any of their new computers. The result is ABM's ability to acquire all sorts of privileged information from a variety of international sources, including governments, businesses and those who use ABM's new computers and have registered their warrantee information.

Someone working for ABM, Bob Rosen, tried to sell the new technology to a competitor and used Ted Ambrose to deliver the chip. Like Ted, he is also murdered, and the sale prevented. ABM's secret is kept secure.

Monika and Andrew, stumble onto this information while searching for evidence to prove ABM's involvement in Andrew's father's murder. As a result they become targets, and ABM tries to stop them from revealing what they have discovered. ABM catches Andrew, but Monika escapes.

Monika manages to notify her boyfriend, James Anstey, a CIA operative working in Los Angeles, via an internet message while she tries to hide from ABM.

James comes to Toronto in an attempt to save Monika from ABM, but is unable to locate her. Eventually he manages to trace her movements and with the aid of the local authorities, manages to find her just in time at the top of the CN Tower, where ABM CEO Arthur Kazinski, is attempting to throw her off the tower. A scuffle ensues. James fights with Kazinski. Shots are fired and Kazinski falls off the tower to his death, 1100 feet below.

Monika is saved by James and later, Andrew is found tied-up and unharmed in ABM's Toronto warehouse. ABM's activities are exposed. James and Monika are reunited. This adventure has made them realize how much they need and love each other.

A NOVEL BY BESTSELLING AUTHOR:
TERENCE MUNSEY

SYNOPSIS

While on vacation, Monika Queller stumbles upon a body and is thrust into a murder-mystery whodunit set along Florida's Gold Coast, from Pompano Beach to Key West, delving into the world of power, politics and cloning…

Monika is to join her fiancé, James Anstey, at the end of the week in Key West, where he is going to take her to meet his parents for the first time. Deciding she wants a few days to explore Florida on her own, she arrives in Miami on a Saturday, rents a car and heads a few miles north to Pompano Beach, planning to work her way down through the Keys and meet James on the following Saturday as they'd agreed. In the meantime, her first stop is the beach.

While on the beach in Pompano, Monika stumbles upon a dead body in the water. She is horrified. The police are called, but the man's body cannot be identified right away. Monika doesn't realize that the dead man is a clone of Dive Master Jesse Ehrlich, that was meant to be disposed of in the ocean and is part of a plot to kidnap the President of the United States.

The kidnapping is being planned by a large computer software company called Microtech and a small group within the military and security forces of the United States. William Fence, CEO of Microtech, along with Major Britin a liaison officer for the military, Cedric Hemings, a Secret Service agent attached to the White House and Dr. Vernon Pearl, are all co conspirators.

In conjunction with the military, Microtech has secretly developed a new method to clone and download all memories and personality of a person. These memories can be uploaded into the clone, creating an almost perfect duplicate that is undetectable to anyone. Moreover, Microtech is able to modify the personality through the upload to make the clone replacement unknowingly do their bidding. The dead body in Pompano was a trial version of the Dive Master to be used in Microtech's scheme. The President is set to attend a ceremony at Fort Jefferson, seventy-eight miles off the coast of Key West. It is there during a dive, that the plot is to unfold.

Monika continues her trip after the experience in Pompano and goes to Key Largo where she hopes to dive at Coral Reef Park. While there, she hires a guide only to discover that he is the exact twin of the dead body she found in the water at Pompano. Monika has discovered a main player in Microtech's conspiracy without realizing it.

The conspirators, who are alerted to Monika's finding of the dead clone in Pompano and the duplicate in Key Largo, chase and capture her. They cannot afford to let her run loose and jeopardize their plans. She is imprisoned in an old abandoned naval base on Key West. While imprisoned, she comes upon the real Jesse Ehrlich who is incarcerated in the cell opposite hers.

Together they unravel the plot against the President. Escaping their imprisonment, Monika tries to contact James but is only able to leave him a message. She and Jesse realize they are now the only ones who can save the President.

Pretending to be part of the media covering the Presidential visit, Monika and Jesse make their way to Fort Jefferson. Once there, they run into a problem and make a startling discovery.